THE FOUR DIAMOND BRAND

A Wild West Novel

THE FOUR DIAMOND BRAND

RANGER LEE

Published for

WILD WEST CLUB

by

HarperCollins*Publishers*

HarperCollins*Publishers*
77–85 Fulham Palace Road
Hammersmith, London W6 8JB
www.harpercollins.co.uk

Paperback edition published by
HarperCollins*Publishers* 2011

1

First published in Great Britain by
Collins Wild West Club 1956

Copyright © Ranger Lee 1956

ISBN 978-0-00-789930-2

Printed and bound in Great Britain by
Clays Ltd, St Ives plc

Find out more about HarperCollins and the environment at
www.harpercollins.co.uk/green

CHAPTER ONE

WAR BETWEEN the Double W and the Circle 22 might have been averted, at least postponed, had not the owners of the two outfits decided to ship their beef from Big Sage the same day. Bill Wallace, who owned the Double W, was sometimes called unkind names by men who did not like him, and they were many. George Villard was often called Villainous Villard, and deservedly.

They were not particular friends, though not sworn enemies as two cattlemen can be when each runs about five thousand head in more or less the same section of the sagebrush country.

Wallace's main range was in the Two Peaks Mountains south of the river, and he had enough hay land in Red Butte Valley, west of the Two Peaks Range, to winter his stock. North of Cottonwood Pass, Villard owned and controlled about fifty square miles of rough range that actually oozed water, and water there meant grass and plenty of grass. Besides this grass he had the run of mountain side where the bunch grass was so high it could have been cut with a mowing machine, had anybody been able to put a mowing machine in that rough country.

Other factors might have kept the peace between Wallace and Villard, had they not stubbornly decided to ship from Big Sage on the same day and in the same number of stock cars. For instance, Wallace had a pretty daughter of marriageable age. Her name was Enid, and Villard had a son name Jim.

Back in their mid-teens at a dance in Big Sage Jim Villard and Enid Wallace had seen and met each other, and despite their adolescence had fallen head over heels in love. They had been that way ever since, Enid now being nineteen and Jim twenty-one, and this in spite of all the opposition to their even meeting. Villard was a hard-headed, hard-shelled, down-east Republican and he said many times he would be eternally damned before he would see his son become the husband of the daughter of a son-of-a-bitch who had strong southern sympathies. Two common characteristics of these two wealthy Nevada cattlemen were avarice for more money, which meant more power and more range, and insane jealousy, picayunishness, and to speak plainly, meanness, though both would have been shocked had they been alluded to as mean. Hell, when a man ran five thousand cattle and had a hundred thousand dollars worth of range, and perhaps fifty thousand dollars in cash, he most certainly could not be mean. Didn't his wealth prove that? Didn't he give at least fifty dollars to charity every year? Didn't he have his riders brand every slick ear he ran across? What was wrong with branding slick ears? Every rancher worth the name did it, in the decade between 1880 and 1890.

On that balmy, fall day George Villard, in a ranch buckboard, was leading the drive of nine hundred and ninety-eight fat beef steers along the broad, sagebrush-bordered trail at the toe of the foothills that slanted down from the north end of Flat Top Mountain.

Yes, there was another factor that might have averted trouble between the two big outfits. This was their determination to keep at least three hard-bitten, gun-slinging, fugitive from justice riders in their crew. Villard had three such men, invariably going armed and at his orders. One of these was Dobie Dick Donovan, tall, raw-boned, rangy, florid of lined face, coppery of hair and moustache. Dobie Dick, along with one of the ordinary riders, was pointing the herd.

This was the last day of their drive and no wagon followed, as Villard had ordered it to proceed to his ten mile long hay ranch on the river and there await orders. That left nine riders with the Circle 22 herd, excepting Villard himself, who in his buckboard could by no stretch of the imagination been called a rider, though he did sit with his fat behind on the sagging seat. Every fall he travelled in that manner with his beef to make sure the riders behind him drove a minimum of fat off the cattle.

They had been on the trail four days, and now, as the slanting sun came down from over the lava-capped summit of Flat Top Mountain, they could see as a dim blur Big Sage little more than ten miles away. Villard unlimbered his ancient field-glasses, and without stopping his slow walking horses, managed to focus them upon Big Sage and then upon the shipping pens. He was immediately jubilant and highly self-satisfied. By the Great Jehovah, there on the spur at the shipping pens was a string of empty cattle cars—his cars, by drab! He would have his nine hundred and ninety-eight fat beef into those cars and ready to be hauled westward before the sun hid itself below the long saddle between the two peaks of the mountain range west of Big Sage.

Out of the sparsely-grassed foothills at the west side of the Two Peaks Range, where the beef cutting had been done, Wallace and his cattle and riders had been on the trail three days. He had nine riders and a chuck wagon which he would take through to Big Sage, load with ranch provisions and send back to ranch headquarters in Red Butte Valley. He, too, was a heavy man, about the same weight as Villard, approximately the same age, between fifty and sixty, but a couple of inches shorter. He, too, invariably travelled in a buckboard when taking his beef to Big Sage for shipping.

Pointing his herd was Brazos Cobb, the wagon boss, and Tom Johnson, one of the ordinary Double W cowboys. Brazos Cobb, short, wiry, even to the point of scrawniness, was wanted in his native state of Texas, and no fewer than two dozen times, three of them being capital offences. But in that decade north central Nevada was a long way from Texas, so the law did not come looking for Brazos Cobb, who, if anything, was an expert cattleman.

He was also a fair hand at handling men. Brazos Cobb, like Dobie Dick Donovan, was seldom seen without being adorned by a filled cartridge belt and a heavy holstered revolver.

At the north end of the Two Peaks Range was a wide, fairly deep swale with an upward surge of land to eastward, which when one is in the swale prevents his getting much of a view of that part of the Humboldt Valley hay land in which Villainous Villard and a few lesser outfits had their home places.

Being about two hundred yards ahead of his point men, Bill Wallace was the first of his outfit to see a slow-moving dust cloud angling in toward Big Sage from the north-east. Had he been half blind in both eyes Wallace would have known instantly that that dust cloud was being made by cattle—yes, by God, by Villard's cattle! What right had he to be heading for Big Sage on the very day the Double W was shipping?

Unlike Villard, Bill Wallace had no field-glasses, no brass tube telescope. He had his voice, however. Stopping his team, he turned sufficiently on the seat to yell loudly for Brazos Cobb, who left the point of the slow-moving herd and went ahead at a trot.

" Yeah, what you want, Bill? " inquired the wagon boss, who could afford to be familiar after working for the Double W for eight years.

Instead of explaining immediately, Wallace actually sat up in his wrath and pointed to that slow-moving dust cloud about ten miles across the valley.

" See that goddamned beef herd, Brazos? " he exploded.

" Sure, I see it. It's Circle 22 stuff, ain't it? What about it? "

" What about it? What about it? " roared Mr. William Wallace, dropping back to the seat with a thud. " Brazos, you named that herd right—it is stuff. Villard, he's so goddamned stingy he won't put good bulls on his range and breed up his cattle—claims there's no money in it. He's nothin' but a goddamned state of Maine farmer, who by all rights should be back there on rocky soil raisin' potatoes."

Brazos Cobb agreed with this because he would agree with anything his employer said, provided he wanted at the moment to agree with him. He reached into an overall pocket and got out a cut of tobacco, gnawed off a chew, masticated a few times and then pushed it into sunken right cheek.

Bill Wallace knew that Villard usually had his field-glasses along. His first reaction to this was one of wrath, guessing, and correctly, that yonder ten miles away Villainous Villard would be watching the progress of the Double W herd.

"You know what, Brazos, that ornery bastard is watching us. I'm going to get me a pair of field-glasses as soon as we hit Big Sage and goin' to watch him. Likely he thinks I'm taking Enid to town with this beef drive so his fine, honourable son James can have another meetin' with her. Damn my hide, if I only had an old telescope along so I could tell if that worthless boy Jim is along with that drive. Brazos, can you tell me with your naked eyes?"

"No, I can't see individual riders," Brazos drawled. "It's just a little too far for my eyesight. It's a safe bet that that boy Jim is along though, it bein' my knowledge that a beef herd hasn't come in from the Circle 22 in five years without that young varmint comin' along. What do you want me to do to him in case I run across him in town—shoot him?"

"No!" Wallace roared. "The young scamp ain't worth it. He is handsome, I got to admit, but just the same he's a Villard—a damned black Republican State of Maine Villard!"

"If you keep in this humour, Bill," Brazos advised, "somebody's goin' to raise hell when they hit town with both outfits there together, Enid not being along. Don't you think you'd better cool down a little?"

In no mild words, Wallace declared that he was not

even thinking of his daughter Enid, he was thinking about the two outfits being in there with their beef, trying to ship on the same afternoon in the same cars. He wound up by declaring that he had ordered forty cattle cars to be at Big Sage on this very day

" Well, maybe Villainous did, too," placated Brazos Cobb, though it could not be said of him that he was not itching for a fight. " There's no law, is there, to keep Villainous from orderin' cars for this day? "

" No, there ain't, but just the same, the way I look at it Villard is shippin' to-day just to tantalize me on account of me objectin' to my handsome and cultured daughter, Enid, wantin' to keep company with his worthless, no-account son. Damn it, what can you see in the direction of Big Sage, which ain't more'n ten miles away? "

Climbing perilously to the unstable seat, Wallace managed to stand there on short, thick, wide-spread legs. He was determined to have as high a coign as his wagon boss, who nonchalantly kept to his saddle. They stared to eastward, and all they could see through shimmering heat veils was a beautiful blue patch, which in his low, drawling voice Brazos said was a damned lie, there not being any lake in that part of Nevada.

" You know it ain't a lake, Brazos, it's one of them meerages. Just my luck for it to settle over where Big Sage should be."

" Oh, Big Sage is still there," Brazos Cobb encouraged. " If you watch it long enough, it'll either disappear, or strange objects, even angel's wings will come out of it. From here you couldn't make out the houses of Big Sage anyway, Bill, so why cuss about it? "

" Because I want a spyglass," said Wallace.

Then his bewhiskered mouth slowly dropped open and remained that way. A house about a hundred feet high, and a little way from it one perhaps seventy-five feet high, came out of the blue mirage. Then one of the railroad water tanks appeared, though about one hundred and fifty feet high.

" My god! " gasped Wallace in actual awe. " There's Jim Morgan's corner store all of a hundred feet high, and I swear it's one story. You know, Brazos, it's the corner brick."

" Optical illusion caused by the reflection of light," drawled Brazos Cobb.

" Keep your scientific terms to yourself, Brazos," Wallace cursed. " I know all about them, but what I'm lookin' for is to see if there's any empties at the shippin' pens. Damn it, Brazos, keep watch. It won't be so bad if there ain't no empties there. In that case Villard and me'll be in the same pickle and can get along friendly like in town."

Wallace was about to climb down in disgust, but not in despair, when in a flash he saw a cattle car about a hundred feet high. He was beginning to take in wind to swear when about apparently a quarter mile from this monstrosity another one shot up into the undulating air. It was perhaps fifty feet high, and of natural length. Then one by one he counted fourteen.

" Count 'em, Brazos, count 'em! " Wallace ordered. " Damnedest things I ever saw! "

Brazos said soberly that he was watching them, but that he was more interested in the shipping pens themselves, which had posts close to a hundred feet high.

" By God, them are my cattle cars there at the pens! " Wallace said triumphantly. " Forty of them should be there. See if you can make out how many there are, Brazos. Let the shipping pens be. We know they're there because they're there all the time."

Brazos presently said that he could count about twenty-five or thirty empties, which, allowing for the spaces between, should number up to forty.

By this time the point of the herd was pressing close up the slope. In his haste to get down from the teetery seat, Bill Wallace almost fell out of the buckboard.

" Ride back pronto to the drag in the flanks, Brazos," he ordered, " and tell the men to speed up their drive a little. Them are my cars and I'm goin' to be the first to fill 'em with cattle!"

"And what if you're not the first, Bill?" Brazos queried as he began to knee his horse around. "What'll we do if Villard gets there first with his beef?"

"What'll we do! What'll we do!" Wallace cursed. "If that Yankee son-of-a-bitch tries to put his beef in my cars, there's goin' to be a fight—that's what we'll do! Hightail it back and tell the riders to get a hustle on with that beef. I'll walk a ton of beef off 'em before I'll let that son-of-a-bitch get those cars. They're my cars—I had 'em ordered for this very afternoon! Damn Yankee! Instead of raisin' cattle out here in Nevada, he should be back in the State of Maine growin' potatoes! Hustle back, Brazos, and tell 'em to double-step these cattle!"

Trotting through the sage at the north side of the straggled, slow-moving herd, Brazos Cobb gave orders to flank and drag men. He came back along the south side telling the flank men there what was to be done.

"Old fool of an idiot!" declared Chunk Carter. "He'll drive a ton of beef off these cattle just to outwit Villard."

"Let him do it, they're his cattle," Brazos Cobb said happily. "I got a hunch there's goin' to be some trouble in town."

"Wouldn't be a bit surprised if there is under these circumstances. How would you like to have a good, old, first-class fight?"

"Reckon we could stand it, if it was a good, old, first-class fight."

On overtaking his employer Brazos saw that Wallace was keeping to the pace of the herd only with the utmost effort. He was red of face, bristling of iron-grey moustache.

"Look at that Villainous Villard," he cursed. "He's speeded up his drive too. I'll horsewhip him if he tries to get them cars first! By God, I will!"

"Well now, Bill," Brazos drawled as he reined alongside the buckboard, " it seems to me if there's goin' to be a fight, somethin' more deadly than horsewhips will be needed or be used. I've heard more'n once how that Dobie Dick Donovan is claimin' how he's goin' to get me sooner or later. Maybe this'll turn out to be the chance for him to do that, one way or the other. Will you begin shootin', Bill, if Villard tries to get them forty cars first? "

" No, I won't," Wallace declared with a blasphemous curse.

CHAPTER TWO

THE TRAVEL of the herd of approximately a thousand is not a thing that can be increased like the opening of the throttle on the locomotive that would haul them to market. They were at the pace they usually travelled, a little better than a mile an hour, and strung out for more than a mile in spite of the efforts of Brazos Cobb and his riders.

To Bill Wallace, under the trying circumstances, this seemed little better than the crawl of a snail. Yonder was the Circle 22 herd across the valley, heading for the shipping pens at Big Sage. To the owner of the Double W, Villard's cattle were travelling at twice the speed of his own herd.

As the Double W herd crawled past Lone Tree Siding, Bill Wallace cursed the railroad for its failure to build shipping pens there. Had the railroad done it, he could have saved nine miles.

He stopped his team, stood up and waved his whip at Brazos Cobb. Seeing the signal, the wagon boss loped ahead.

" What you want, Bill? If we push those beef any faster, the lard on the fat ones will melt like butter in the sun. We're travellin' too fast now."

" Who the hell's runnin' this outfit, Cobb? Don't expect you to get more speed out of 'em. I've decided

I'm goin' to head for town and see to it I get them forty empties. That son-of-a-bitch Villard will steal 'em if he gets a chance. What do you think of that plan, Brazos?"

"Better do it," Cobb agreed. "You ain't doin' any good joggin' along there ahead of the drive. Go ahead and corral them empties so Villard's outfit can't get 'em."

"The hell I ain't doin' any good!" Wallace swore. "Who's runnin' this big outfit? Who's the executive? Who's tendin' to all the business? Don't tell me I ain't doin' any good. Who sees to it that you men get paid without waitin'?"

"Now keep your shirt on, Bill," the gunman advised calmly. "Tell you what, you drive ahead, Bill. Villard will likely think of the same thing and when you both get to town about the same time, fight it out for them empty cars, and have it all settled by the time we reach the pens with the cattle."

For about a minute Wallace didn't like that suggestion, then he saw it as just the opportunity for which he'd been waiting for years. He'd hammer George Villard's face until the owner of the Circle 22 couldn't even see out of one eye. They were about the same age, about the same weight.

Wallace started to get under way in a hurry, then changed his mind. Something he should have kept in his mind all the time had slipped. He got it back with a rush and saw possible new angles to the coming trouble.

"Brazos, ain't this the day Enid was going to head for Big Sage across the short-cut mountain trail, ain't it?"

"This is the day," agreed Brazos Cobb, secretly happy at the prospect of more trouble. "If she left early, she'll be well up toward the summit by this time—maybe goin' down the east side. Why? Wasn't it planned she'd have a nice time in town with some of her friends, and be there on hand to see us load this beef? You ain't begrudgin' Enid that pleasure, are you, Bill?"

"No!" Wallace growled. "But just the same, I think she'd been a damned sight better off if she'd stayed at home, especially if Jim Villard, the worthless young reprobate, is with that drive yonder. I ain't agoin' to tolerate no meetin' between them two. Push the cattle along at moderate speed. I'll cinch those empties in town. There ain't no sense in drivin' off too much weight. Have the beef there in time to load before sundown."

Across the valley, on the slowly shortening base of the triangle, George Villard had reached much the same decision as the angry and impatient owner of the Double W had reached under the high pressure of hate, envy and jealousy. The crawl of the herd was much too slow. He would drive ahead and get possession of those empty cattle cars. Why shouldn't he? They were his empties, weren't they?

"Well, I don't know about that," said Donovan. "Wallace bringin' in his beef to-day looks to me like he might have ordered some empties too."

"Well, if he has, the dratted varmint can't have 'em! I ordered my cars two weeks ago from this very day, and by God, there they are over on the other side of the shippin' pens on the spur. If Wallace, the damned old thievin' reprobate, gets hold of those empties first, he'll fill 'em with his cattle, and where'll I be?"

At this moment, Jim Villard, who had been riding at point with Donovan, trotted ahead and stopped where his father and Dobie Dick were conferring at the buckboard. He said that in his opinion the cattle were already being pushed much too fast. Had his father lost his head?

"Son, you'll lose yours if you don't keep from meddlin' with our business," Villainous Villard retorted. "See that dust cloud yonder and off to west? That's the Double W herd comin' in. It's just one of Bill Wallace's lowdown tricks. Over yonder at the shippin' pens are my forty empties, for these very cattle."

"But maybe Wallace ordered empties, too, for to-day," Jim argued. "He's got a right to do that, ain't he?"

"He ain't got any dratted right to be shippin' on the

same day I'm shippin'!" Villard exploded. "He knows that as well as I do. It's just another of his damned tricks to pester me—that dratted varmint, I'll pester him!"

"Yes, the way you're actin', Pap, I think you will," Jim Villard drawled. "But here's something maybe you overlooked. Did Wallace know we were going to ship to-day? His ranch headquarters are at least fifty miles from ours. If I was you, Pap, I wouldn't get too mad about this business until we find out whether there'll be two strings of forty cars each waitin' there for us at Big Sage."

Jim Villard was tall, lithe, handsome, too. He was not over proud of being the son of George Villard, but he was extremely proud of being able to ride anything that wore hair and stood on four hoofs, and being in love with Enid Wallace, and having her in love with him, and, yes—of his first full-grown, slender blond moustache! He was also proud of his ability as a fighter, not that he had had to date more than a dozen serious scraps.

Guessing at what was in his son's mind, George Villard smiled at him, brandished a whip, told him that if the Wallace girl were in town he was to stay strictly away from her.

This put the possibility of Enid being in town into Jim's mind, and his heart thumped. He did not, however, lose his temper because he knew that he had more than one way of fooling the old man.

"But, Pap, what makes you think Miss Enid will be in Big Sage?" he queried with forced intimacy. "I ain't set eyes on her since calf roundup. Did she send you word she'd be in Big Sage to-day?"

It was not often that George Villard profaned the name of the Deity, his reasoning being that such profanation would eventually doom him to hell's fire. He swore now, ending with——

"No, she didn't send me any word she'd be in Big Sage, Jim. If she had I wouldn'ta believed her. That girl's no good! She's just a designin' female! How could she be any good with Bill Wallace her father? Don't you argue or talk back to me! I'll tell you plain what I'm goin' to do. If you get to minglin' with that Enid girl in town, if she's there . . ."

"But dammit, man, there isn't one chance in a thousand she'll be there so why get all riled up about it now?"

"Don't you cuss me, you young scamp!" Villard warned, waving the whip again. "You ain't so big yet that I can't larrup you. Get back to the point and keep those cattle on the move. Dobie, you go with him. I built the Circle 22 up to what it is, and, by drat, I still should have enough sense left to keep Bill Wallace from gettin' those empty cars! Mind you, Jim——"

"Yes, sir," prompted the tall, blond young rider as his features tightened and lost colour. "What are you goin' to tell me?"

"What am I goin' to tell you? I'm goin' to tell you that if Wallace gets those empty cars, and you find his daughter there and have any truck with her, I'm goin' to take my men and use all my money if necessary and run him out of the Two Peaks Range. He don't own five hundred acres of land in it, anyway. He's just runnin' on government land."

"Well, and ain't that what you're doin', George, yourself?" queried Donovan. "In fact, I doubt that you yourself own more'n a thousand acres outright of all the big range you run your cattle on."

Dobie Dick Donovan was secretly thrilling at the prospect of a real fight—one in which guns could be used. Hell, since he'd been wagon boss for the Circle 22 he hadn't actually had a good gunfight. There were two or three Wallace men, including that scrawny runt of a Brazos Cobb, that he'd like to match guns with. Hadn't Brazos Cobb sent word to him that no goddamned Irishman could be a gunfighter?

Seeing that his son and the range boss made no move to go, Villard became even angrier at them. Though he did want to curse, he gritted his teeth and told them to get back to the point.

"Sure, in a minute or two, George," declared Dobie Dick Donovan. "Now, in case Wallace gets his mad up and tries to invade your range, what are you going to do?"

"What am I goin' to do? What am I goin' to do? Let the thievin' varmint come! I'll make him and his outfit so sick they'll turn tail and get clean out of Nevada —that's what I'll do! It had to come sooner or later, so let it come now. By drat, I'm a law-abidin', patriotic Yankee,. and I ain't forgot there was a Civil War. In my opinion, Donovan, all such men as Bill Wallace should either have been shot at the end of the war or imprisoned for life. Are you goin' to keep them cattle movin'?"

"The cattle are movin', Pap," reminded Jim. "It won't be long until the point of 'em is pushin' you out of the road unless you get to movin'. It seems to me——"

"Yes, what seems to you, son?" interrupted his indignant father.

"It seems to me, Pap," Jim drawled, "you're crossin' your bridge of trouble a long way before you get to it."

That reminded Villainous Villard of something he had overlooked in his rage. He had a herd of nearly a thousand cattle, all ranging from half wild to wild. Drat it all holler! He'd lose time with his herd getting across that dratted bridge that spanned the river. He'd lose valuable minutes there.

Why in tarnation hadn't he started the drive earlier this morning? Why hadn't he pressed the cattle a little faster? There was but one thing to do to thwart Bill Wallace—that was to reach Big Sage before Wallace did, and get possession of those forty empties on the spur at the shipping pens. He lashed his mustangs with a whip. They went into their collars so abruptly that they almost cracked Villard's spine as he was slapped against the back of the buckboard seat. Grimacing with momentary pain, he pulled the horses down to a swift trot.

" Well, lad, what are you going to do if Miss Enid proves to be in town?" queried Dobie Dick Donovan as he rode slowly back to reach the point of the slowly advancing herd. " Would you add further complications to the troubles of your old man? "

" Troubles be damned! " Jim swore, as his jaw muscles corded. " He ain't happy unless he's in trouble. What am I goin' to do if Enid's in town? I'm goin' to court her, of course. Here's somethin' my father's overlooked. He doesn't realise that I'm free, white and twenty-one, and by God, Enid Wallace is a good girl! "

" And that," said the gun-fighting wagon boss, " will further add to the troubles of your old man. Are you dead set on marryin' Miss Enid, if she'll have you? "

" Have me? Have me? Hell, Dobie, she's told me more'n once that she'll have me, and by God, I'm ready to have her! "

" It may start a range war," Donovan said, as he and Jim stopped their horses to let the point come slowly up. " Less things than that have started big range trouble."

In his present mood, which included the yearning for considerable hard liquor, Dobie Dick Donovan did not much care where or what trouble was so long as it came. He hadn't smoked up a gun for a considerable time. Still, being a Circle 22 man, he wanted to see the Circle 22 get those forty empty cars. Offsetting this wish a little was his distinct liking for Jim Villard. Jim wasn't much like his old man. He was just the sort of a young puncher a handsome young lady should rightfully fall in love with.

" Look at the old man and his rig raisin' dust! " Dobie Dick said and chuckled. " He's tryin' to tear up the whole road, ain't he? "

" Yes, he's raisin' dust," Jim agreed calmly. " If he gets in there and starts trouble with Bill Wallace, I'm afraid he's goin' to raise so much hell he won't have blocks enough to prop it up with."

As Jim turned his horse to take the direction of the slow travelling herd, he sighed and said to himself:

" I wonder if by any chance Enid will be in town to-day? Doggone it, I'd sure like to hold her in my arms again and give her a few kisses. My father, he's as full of hate as a locoed jack-rabbit, but he can't bust up this business between Enid and me."

Whatever it is that shapes the lives of foolish men had so arranged it that bright October day as to have George Villard and William Wallace arrive in Big Sage within a space of sixty seconds. The pretty, grey-eyed daughter of one of them, clad in a buckskin riding suit and on a buckskin horse, was descending the easterly foothills of the Two Peaks Range preparatory to striking out across about four miles of grey sage flats toward town.

She had with her the pleasant suspicion that with the Circle 22 herd coming in across the river was a certain young rider she'd like very much to see again. She had this thought with the vague belief that there would be trouble in town as she could see her father's herd coming slowly and patiently in from the west. From her slightly elevated position she could also see a string of empty cattle cars on the spur at the shipping corrals.

Clattering across the railroad tracks just east of the water tank, George Villard turned sharply to his right. A drunk cowboy yelled loudly:

" Why you comin' so fast for a doctor, Villard? Your wife's too old to have another baby, ain't she? You got them horses of yours all in a lather and a sweat."

Villard cursed him but kept going, hauling his sweat-lathered mustangs to a stop close to the back of the railroad station where four boys were busily engaged in a game of marbles.

At this moment Bill Wallace of the Double W had finished tying his sweat-lathered team to the board-fence that surrounded the spare ground of the Empire Hotel, which was at the north side of the track. He had seen Villard coming and was determined to beat him into the railroad depot. He had proof that these forty empties were his cars.

Blowing perceptibly because of the long, hard ride, Wallace waddled across the track, and was heading for the front door of the station when around the corner rushed Villard. They stopped, bristled, growled like two surprised, but nevertheless belligerent bulldogs. Wallace was the first to find voice, he said:

" What the hell are you doin' here in town, Villard? If you're tryin' to get them forty empty stock cars on the spur up yonder, they're mine! Go buy yourself a drink, if you ain't too stingy."

" By drat, Wallace, I seldom drink and you know that!" Villard panted. " As for them empties bein' yours, they're mine—they're forty empties I ordered for to-day to ship my cattle in. Go crawl in a badger hole and pull the hole in after you, you dratted rebel of a man! "

There was enough more of this to draw Wes Moreland, the youngish, fattish agent, into the doorway. He said hello to the two men, but was completely ignored.

" Come and take a look, Fred," Moreland said to the day trick telegraph operator. " We've got a couple of toothless old badgers in town and they're about to spring on each other."

Spitting on his hands, rubbing them together, making gnarled fists out of them and hunching his middle-aged shoulders, Wallace ordered Villard to come on.

The owner of the 22 was about to begin obeying when he surveyed Moreland in the doorway with Fred, the telegraph operator, pressing past him.

" Howdy, Wes," Villard panted. " Ain't them my forty empties yonder by the shipping pens? They are, of course."

" Your empties, hell! " cursed Wallace. " They're my cars! I ordered forty empties for to-day. Didn't I, Wes? "

" Sure, you did, Mr. Wallace," agreed the agent.

" And by drat, I did, too—I mean I ordered forty cars for to-day! " roared Villard. " Didn't I order forty empty stock cars for to-day, Moreland? "

" Yes, you did," agreed Moreland, suppressing a smile.
" But only forty empties have come in, gentlemen."

" And said forty empties are my cars," Villard growled
triumphantly.

" Which makes you a damned liar, Villard! " Wallace
corrected. " Them forty are my cars. Wes here knows it,
ain't that so, Wes? "

" I'll be hanged if I know, gentlemen," said the agent.
" Only forty has come in, but the other forty should be
along any hour. Is there such a demand for beef down at
the coast you got to have those forty other empties this
split second? "

" Split second be hanged! " roared Villard, who wanted
very much to profane the Deity. " It ain't a matter of
demand for beef, it's a matter of justice. Ain't you got
no record of who those forty empties are for, Moreland? "

Villard had no more than said that when he began
shivering with fright lest Moreland say the forty cars
belonged to Wallace. Moreland turned to the telegraph
operator and said:

" Fred, who do those forty empties belong to? You
signed for them, didn't you, yesterday while I was at
dinner! "

" Yes, I signed for them, yesterday noon when the westbound local freight pushed them there on the siding. All
the tag called for was forty empty stock cars. I don't
know who they belong to."

" There, by drat, of all the slipshod methods of doin'
business! " Villard stormed self-righteously. " And for a
big operatin' railroad to do a thing like that—makin' no
note of whether them were the forty empties I ordered.
By a matter of justice, they're my empties, and by the
great Jehovah, I'm goin' to load my cattle into them! "

" And by hell, you're not, Villard! " corrected Wallace,
as his big gnarled fists opened and closed. " Them are
my forty empties and I'm goin' to load my beef into 'em,
come hell or high water! Yonder is my beef comin' down
yonder, where you see that dust—close to a thousand

head of 'em. I'm a first-class customer of this here railroad. If Fred there signed for forty empty stock cars, by God they're my stock cars! "

It occurred to Moreland then that he might placate these two belligerents, though he did wish to see them fight. He began by saying that the westbound freight should be along within an hour and that it would beyond doubt have forty empty stock cars, which it would push on a siding while the other forty were being loaded.

" With whose cattle? " Villard interrupted. " With my cattle, of course. I'm goin' to put my cattle into those empties now."

" Which you sure ain't," disagreed Wallace. " I'm goin' to load my beef into those forty empties, or I'm goin' to bust a gut, Villard. Go find yourself a big badger hole and crawl into it, you damned blue-nosed, blue-bellied Yankee! Tell you what I'll do to show you just what sort of a sport you are. I'll cut you at cards or shake you at dice or spit at a mark, Villard, to decide which of us take those forty empty stock cars. Come on, I dare you to. Speakin' of guts, you ain't got guts enough to take a chance, Villard."

" I ain't! I ain't! " roared the owner of the Circle 22 and then discovered that he never gambled except on sure things. " It's one of your low-down, rebel tricks, Wallace. You know I ain't a gamblin' man."

" Sure, I know that," Wallace sneered. " Just as well as I know you'd steal one of my beef that wasn't branded. Since you won't gamble, do you want to fight? Come on, if you want to mix it with me. That won't be no gamble for me to take because I'll knock you so damned galley-west you won't think of stock cars for a week! "

" Sic 'em! Sic 'em! " advised Fred, the telegraph operator. " Go to it, men, and settle it that way. Don't you think they'd better, Wes? "

" Sure, let 'em settle it that way," agreed Moreland. " I don't actually know who has first claim to those forty empties. Let 'em settle it to suit themselves."

"Then, by God, they're my empties," Wallace declared happily as he prepared to rush. "It'll take me about half a minute to prove that."

"And your half a minute will be about half an hour, Wallace, you damned old rebel reprobate!" Villard cursed happily. "And when that half minute's ended, I'll be walkin' on your face and takin' them forty cars. Come on, you damned rebel cattle thief, if you've got a grain of sand in that gizzard your call your fightin' heart! I ain't had a good fight since I marched with Sherman. Don't you turn tail and run, Wallace, which I know by your cowardly nature you want to do. Stand up and fight! I'm comin' to you!"

"And I'm comin' to you, Villard!" chuckled the owner of the Double W, "and I'm comin' in a hurry!"

CHAPTER THREE

HERE WAS SOMETHING new for Big Sage—wealth engaged in serious combat with wealth. The less fortunate enjoyed this so wholeheartedly that within a space of a minute fifty of them were gathered for an audience and more were coming. Wallace, swinging widely, but with deadly intent, landed the first real blow. It crashed against the left side of Villard's high-arched nose, giving it, as time was to prove, a perceptible list to starboard.

"There, you damned Yankee! That'll learn you I know how to fight," Wallace panted.

More by accident than by design, Villard shot out a straight punch that landed against Wallace's mid-section. Wallace's mouth flew open and out of it gushed all the air in his lungs, taking with it a wet spray of tobacco juice that doused the furious countenance of Villard.

Then the fighting really began, because as he punched and swung, Villard accused Wallace of insulting him by spitting in his face, and worse than that, spitting tobacco juice. They grappled and tried to trip each other. They panted and they swore. One spectator sized it up in this manner:

" When it comes to sense, they ain't got none of it, have they? I once saw a couple of drunk Injuns put on the same kind of a fight, except they got to workin' with knives. Pound him in the guts, Villard, that's his weak point! "

Villard tried to do this, but in return got a clout to the jaw that rocked his greying head so far to the right that he actually heard his neck joints crack. He wanted to grab his head and straighten it up, but he didn't have the time. He pushed out his straight right, apparently his favourite and one serviceable blow. He collided again with Wallace's mid-section. This time Wallace let out a string of oaths instead of a spray of tobacco juice.

" Now, you Yankee varmint, I'm goin' to kill you, because I ain't used to bein' hit twice in the same place! " Wallace swore and fought more furiously.

Villard also fought more furiously, but still more clumsily. He suddenly ceased swinging and punching. Each got a crotch hold, and each, on lifting, intending to throw his adversary anywhere, discovered that it was much like trying to lift himself by his own bootstraps.

" Break! " a man ordered. " This here ain't no damned wrestlin' match. Break, or we'll pull you two old goats apart! "

" Goats! " a man derided. " They're just a pair of old stags! Two damned bad they ain't got horns."

They broke, and Villard swung, and whether he intended to do so or not, Wallace ducked. His broad hat was knocked off. To prove he was deadly and meant it, Villard jumped on the hat and stamped on it, but this almost proved his undoing because Wallace climbed him from behind, bore him down and almost rooted his face in the gravel, when with an upheaval Villard overturned him and got on top. He was drawing back to begin the full disfigurement of Wallace's face, when the owner of the Double W reared up at the feet, putting all his weight on his broad, muscular shoulders. He swung Villard over his head, but scramble as he would, was not in time to land on top of the owner of the Circle 22.

"Gouge eyes!" a man yelled. "Gouge eyes! Anything's fair in this kind of a fight."

"Don't forget to bite ears, too," another man called. "Bite the rich son-of-a-bitch, Wallace. Make a crop and underbit out of his right ear!"

Enid's furious father was trying to do just this when Villard, with a snap of jaws, caught nothing more than a mouthful of Wallace's whiskers.

Wallace quickly dislodged this grip by stripping both both hands down along his whiskers and not gently, thus forcing Villard's grip to slip. They scrambled to their feet, backed off to get their wind, thrust at each other like two crazed bulls. Their bare heads collided with a thump and slowly they settled to the ground.

"One, two, three, four, five," a hilarious onlooker began to count. "Hell, why should this count be made? They're both out!"

Joe Hitchcock, who ran the Empire Hotel, came with a pail of water, which he flung upon Villard's inert face. To show there was no partiality here a man ran and got a pail of water with which to drench Wallace from crotch to the top of his iron-grey thatch. The cold water had no effect on either man, but for their quick breathing they might have been dead.

"What happened, men?" demanded old Dr. Latchford, the town's physician, who had just arrived. "I didn't hear any shooting. I see no blood to indicate knife work."

"Oh, they just had a bull fight, Doc," said Hitchcock. "It was the case of the Bull of Bashan collidin' with that old Durham—we used to call him Bill Wallace. They hit head on, each full tilt."

"Frontal bones of their foreheads?" interrogated Latchford, who was more than half drunk as usual.

"No, the tops of their heads, Doc," a man shouted. "They came full tilt at each other and collided head on. If they'da had horns, you coulda heard them a-rattlin' and a-clashin' all the way to the bridge. What you suppose is the matter with 'em, Doc? Do you suppose they got fractured skulls?"

"Hell, no, not them two!" Dr. Latchford said, trying to be very professional. "It'll turn out to be nothing more than dual example of concussion. They'll come to in due time. A couple of you men get a couple of buckets of cold water and trickle it on their heads. If they've got any brains, the brains may be a little damaged but it'll be all right. I just pulled out of a big poker game over there at the Silver State because of all this racket, and by God, this is all it amounts to! If they die, notify me, and I'll see they get buried."

In obedience to Latchford's orders, a couple of men got as many buckets of cold water, and each squatting, trickled water upon an unconscious man's head.

"Pour some on old Wallace's face," a man advised. "In case some of that gets into his lungs that'll make him snort himself to. Go ahead, you can't drown him. Hey, you, Jake, try that on Villard, too. He's got a bloody nose and you can at least wash off the blood."

Instead of trickling the water on the unconscious men's faces, the men with the buckets actually dumped them, each pail being about two-thirds full. Wallace revived with a sputtering snort, a gasp, a choke. He pawed at his face. He muttered unintelligible curses. He rolled over and managed to get to all fours, his head hanging low, and at that moment if he'd had a tail it would have been dragging on the ground.

"Hold his head up, somebody," a man advised. "He's goin' to puke."

"Where's that Yankee son-of-a-bitch that butted me like a bull?" Wallace demanded when he could find words. "It ain't fair fightin', but it's no more than you can expect from him. Where is he?"

In the meantime Villard had come to a little more slowly and with a little more dignity, but sitting there on the wet gravel, he looked like anything but a dignified wealthy rancher.

Villard patted the top of his dripping head and groaned, alternating the groans with mumbles, which if interpreted meant that he was deploring the fact that he had engaged in combat with a thing that he thought a man, but which had turned out to be a bull.

" But, Villainous," Hitchcock reminded. " You butted him."

" I didn't do no such thing, Hitchcock," bawled the owner of the Circle 22. " I was just grapplin' with him, meanin' to throw him and walk on him when the fool slipped and I slipped and our heads collided—bull fight a rebel like him! Somebody lend me a gun. By drat, with a gun I'll make short work of him."

" You'll do what? " roared Wallace, as he scrambled to his feet and tottered. " Why, you damned bull-fightin' Yankee, I'll walk on you, and as for you handlin' a gun, Villard, you got to hire your gunfightin' done 'cause you don't know which end the bullet comes out of."

" I don't? I don't? " Villard panted as he began to get to his feet. " Talk about me hirin' my shootin' done, what about you, Wallace. What about that outlaw, Brazos Cobb, who rode your outfit? What about him? "

" Best goddamned cowman in Nevada, and best fighter, too! " Wallace shouted. " While your talkin' about gunmen, what about your prize package as calls himself Dobie Dick Donovan? He brags around he's got seven notches on his gun, and the lord only knows how many more he didn't cut there because he was ashamed of 'em—them lives bein' Mexicans and Injuns. What about some of your other men? I ain't namin' names, but everybody in the country knows who I mean. Let me loose, men, I want to walk him down. Damn his thievin' heart, claimin' them forty empty stock cars are his when he knows damned well they ain't. I ordered forty empties for this afternoon and Wes Moreland will tell you I did. Didn't I, Wes? "

" Yes, you did," the railroad agent admitted, suppressing a smile. " I've got your order on file inside."

" And by God," yelled Wallace after he had slapped his thighs with his hand and crowed like a rooster, " them forty empties up there at the loadin' chute are mine, by God, and I'd like to see the colour of the man's eyes who says they ain't."

" I say they ain't. They ain't! " yelled Villard, who was being held by four men. " Them forty empties on the spur up there are mine, and when my cattle arrive they're goin' to be loaded into them same cars."

" Over my dead body, you damned lyin' Yankee! "

" And over my dead body, you dratted lowdown, ornery rebel! If you load your beef into those cars, Wallace, it'll be over my dead body and over the dead bodies of all my loyal men."

" Includin' your son Jim? " an onlooker demanded. " Are you goin' to have him killed in this silly business too, Villard? "

" By drat, I will, that is if he found he was needed to defend the body and the honour of his father. He's my son, by drat, and he'll fight to the last drop of his blood for his father."

" Damned if I believe that, Villard," Hitchcock drawled. " If it's true, though, I haven't got much respect for your son's judgment. Let 'em loose, men, and let's see what they'll do. I'm layin' three to one on Wallace puttin' him out inside the next ten minutes."

" By God, let me loose," panted Wallace, who was actually frothing at the mouth. " Let me at him! By God, I'm mad enough at him now to take him apart in such little pieces he can't be put back together again. Let me loose, you men, or I'll kick backwards and break your shins."

The three men released him in a split second before

the four men released Villard. The antagonists swayed a little, regained their balance and rushed, heads down again, but before their heads could collide, the burly, middle-aged bodies that owned these heads were grappled and the adversaries pulled back, Wallace cursing and Villard mouthing righteously that the avenging hand of the Lord would sooner or later fall with devastating effect upon one William Wallace.

" Quit your preachin', Villard! " Wallace yelled.

Seeing that the adversaries could be restrained without difficulty, two men brought as many chairs from the railroad office and Villard and Wallace were seated upon them.

" Gentlemen, court is now convened," Hitchcock said soberly. " Go ahead and state your case. The trouble is, who's the plaintiff and who's the defendant? This is most perplexin'."

" Hell, there ain't nothin' legal about it. Suppose we let Villard talk first. Villainous, what have you got to say for yourself? "

Villard was still so enraged that he failed to hear the epithet attached to his name. He turned irately, yet entreatingly, to Moreland and said:

" Wes, now as an honest man speaking to honest men, weren't those forty cattle cars up there on the spur consigned to me? "

" Mr. Villard, I'll be damned if I know," the agent said honestly. " I sent in orders for eighty cattle cars to be delivered here to-day and that consignment of forty came in yesterday, and they may be for you, and yet again they may be for Mr. Wallace. You're both good shippers here for the company and I can't take sides."

" Wes, by God, you don't need to take sides," broke in Wallace. " Them's my cars and you know it. I'm loadin' my beef into 'em just as soon as my beef arrive. Any objection to that, Wes? "

" No objection to that," said the agent. " First come, first served. Seems to me that'd be the best way to settle this problem. The first man to get one car loaded with his beef has the right to load the other thirty-nine cars with his beef. Will that meet with your approval, Mr. Villard?"

"No, it don't! By drat, it don't! I got to use those forty empties for my cattle, or I'll sue this railroad. Get out your records, Moreland, and I'll prove those forty cars were consigned to me."

Really enjoying himself, Moreland confessed that the only record he had of the forty empties was the acceptance signed by Fred Bailey, the previous noon.

"Oh my, oh my," Villard groaned righteously, spacing his words with clucks back of his jolted up teeth. "What a slippery slip-shod method for a great railroad company to indulge in—makin' a memorandum of forty empty cattle cars without notin' down the name of the man to whom they were consigned. Shut up, Wallace, I'm talkin'!"

"And sayin' nothin' as usual," Wallace said with a snort. "Put a gag on your talk, Villard, and everybody will feel better."

Though the erstwhile combatants showed no inclination to again rise from their chairs and engage in mortal combat, they could not be choked off when it came to talk. They talked and they argued and they threatened. Villard was appealing to Moreland for the ninth time to bring forth proof showing that the forty empties were consigned to him when Fred Bailey, the day trick operator, hurried out waving a yellow paper. He called for silence and read:

"Division Freight Office, Ogden, Utah. Eighty empty cattle cars left for Big Sage, Nevada, per schedule, forty in each lot. One forty consigned to William Wallace, the other forty to George Villard. Have no record of which forty arrived there first. According to advice from Elko and Winnemucca, second forty cars should arrive in Big Sage not later than six, this p.m."

"That proves this forty is for me, don't it, Villard?"

crowed Wallace, " me bein' in this country a little longer than you."

Again they talked, they argued, they swore, they threatened. The spectators talked, of course, advising, ridiculing, encouraging another fight, but Villard and Wallace talked on even going as far as threatening to cut each other's throats. Time passed, and then more time, and the white ball of autumn sun sank lower, then lower behind the long saddle that coupled up the two rounded basalt strewn peaks that gave the mountain range its name.

" Say, yonder comes a herd of bawlin' cattle in from the west," a man shouted.

" They're my cattle! Whose else cattle could they be comin' in from the west? " Wallace shouted triumphantly as he rose stiffly from his chair. " My cattle are ahead of Villards. Now I got a right to load 'em into those cars, ain't I, Wes? "

" Yes, you can load if you get your cattle in the pens first," said the agent. " I don't see any way out of it. It seems to me fair play."

Villard was about to protest this decision when from the direction of the river came a dull roar like the far-off trampling of many hoofs on an unstable plank floor.

It was the roar made by the leaders of the Circle 22 herd as it was stampeded across the river bridge by six shots fired over the backs by Dobie Dick Donovan.

" Keep 'em goin', boys, keep 'em goin'! " Donovan yelled as he began to reload to be prepared for real trouble in town. " Don't push 'em too hard."

Knowing that this rush of cattle would occur, Jim Villard had ridden ahead and taken a stand about a hundred yards up the dusty road, where he soon began to turn the cattle slightly to the right so they could take a straight line toward the shipping pens.

Despite his still aching head, Villard knew what that rumble meant—his cattle were crossing the bridge. He got quickly to his feet, but he rose no more quickly than did Wallace. Wallace said:

" Excuse me, gents, I'll be goin' down to the shippin' pens to supervise the loadin' of my beef."

" By drat, I don't need the likes of you to supervise the loadin' of my beef, Wallace! " Villard stormed. " I'm quite capable of doin' that myself. Stay where you are. My herd's goin' to arrive first, and them are my empties. Stay where you are unless you want to get into serious trouble. My patience has absolutely run out with you."

" Well, so has mine, gentlemen," spoke up long, lanky, grizzled Sheriff Andy Smith, who had been an almost silent spectator and listener. " I'll just amble along with you two to make sure there ain't no further hostilities down at the pens. Come along, you two fools, one of you walk on each side of me."

Before these three and a considerable part of the crowd could get into motion, a young woman in bright calico darted around a corner of the depot, breathing hard, searching the crowd for somebody. She uttered a happy gasp as she espied Bill Wallace, owner of the Double W. She rushed upon him, flung herself into his arms, wrapped her arms about his neck and in a forced panting whisper said:

" Mr. Wallace, she's at my house. She just rode in. She's going to stay with me while she's in town. Do you mind, Mr. Wallace? I told her I'd come and tell you she was here."

" Who's here? Who's here? " Wallace panted as he managed to release her arms. " Who's here, Lottie Edwards? Who're you talkin' about? My God in heaven, is that fool girl of mine here in town? "

" Yes, she is! Yes, she is! " Lottie panted. " Do you mind if she stays with me while she's in town? She's a little bit bunged up from ridin' so hard over the mountain. You won't mind, will you, Mr. Wallace? Enid's awful tired, and Mama and me got her to lay down for a little while. Do you mind? "

Answering her with a grunt and a nod, Wallace turned wrathfully upon his erstwhile adversary to whom he snarled:

"Say, Villainous Villard, is that worthless no-account son of yours with you with that herd? I want to know that."

"Yes, by drat, he is, and what are you goin' to do about it?" snorted the owner of the Circle 22. "My son Jim come in with the herd and he's goin to supervise the loadin' of my cattle, and I don't want any more trouble out of you, Wallace."

"Well, I'm goin' to supervise the loadin' of my cattle," Wallace declared, "and, Sheriff, I don't need you, either."

"Well, maybe you don't," drawled the sheriff, "but I'm goin' just the same. Seems to me I smell trouble."

"And I'm goin' also, by drat," declared Villard, "and when I get to the pens, I'm goin' to supervise the loadin' of my beef, come what may. Sheriff Smith, you can't say me nay."

"I ain't agoin' to neigh at you, Villainous," the sheriff said very soberly. "Horses do that. Come along, if you're so minded, but I'm warnin' you, I ain't agoin' to tolerate no more fightin' between you and Wallace!"

CHAPTER FOUR

THE REACTION of the ordinary cowboy to the shipping of cattle is similar to that of a seasoned fire horse when he hears an alarm. There were, that fall afternoon, an even twenty cowboys in from smaller ranches and a few from outfits of their own. About half of these were half drunk, and with them and the sober riders, the fight between the two wealthy ranchers was cause enough for unusual excitement.

Then they espied the two herds angling in from

different directions. There was an immediate stampede for saddled horses left at the hitching rails along the short main street. Hoofs were soon pounding toward the pens, where, by this time, Bill Wallace was standing on one side of the open gate, George Villard at the other. Now fully fifty people, mostly men, but enough women and children, were perched upon the fence at each side. Now, if there's any real help in getting half wild cattle into a corral it's to have the fence lined with human beings, especially by a few women in gaudy calico or red woollen dresses.

"Folks, if you want to help pen these cattle," the sheriff said, "get down off that fence. You kids, get off the cars, too. Absent yourselves over there in the direction of the depot. Give these steers a chance."

The majority reluctantly obeyed; the minority did not despite the sheriff's repeated order. Then the twenty cowboys, riding hard, straggled in from Main Street. Seeing them, Villard shouted:

"A dollar in hard cash for each man that helps pen my beef. You can't make a dollar any easier, boys."

Before the twenty riders could make up their minds about that, Bill Wallace yelled that he'd pay two dollars. Then before the score of riders could head toward the oncoming Double W herd, Villard shouted that he'd pay three dollars per man.

"Four dollars, you old buzzard!" yelled Wallace. "Four dollars hard cash to each man. Sheriff Andy Smith will make good my word."

"No, I won't, Bill," the sheriff shouted. "I'm keepin' out of this muddle unless there's fightin'."

"Five dollars for each man who helps!" bellowed Villard. "Five dollars cold cash. Where can you riders make five dollars easier? You tell me!"

"Six dollars!" shouted Wallace. "Six dollars cold, hard cash for each man who helps pen my beef."

That was to start a wild stampede for the oncoming Double W herd, when Villard yelled that he'd pay six dollars and fifty cents.

"Seven dollars and a half," shouted Wallace. "Villard, you old stingy guts, you ain't a sport if you don't raise more'n a half dollar. I'm biddin' seven and a half. What's your bid?"

"Eight dollars!" shouted Villard, who was beginning to multiply twenty by eight with the result that he got the price of about four good steers.

"Nine dollars and twenty-five cents for every man who helps pen my cattle first!" shouted Villard. "You men get the money just as soon as the gates close on my beef. Where in tarnation can you make nine dollars and a quarter easier?"

"Ten dollars flat!" bellowed Bill Wallace. "Now you waddies, tell me where you could pick up a ten easier than that—like pickin' it out of the sagebrush."

Villard started to raise that but changed his mind because ten times twenty spelled two hundred dollars, and two hundred dollars to George Villard wasn't chicken-feed. Villard was now taunted by Wallace, by half the town, judging by the noise scores of shrill voices made.

"Won't do it! Won't do it!" Villard shouted righteously. "Ain't gonna be imposed on. Wallace, by tarnation, if you keep me from shippin' my beef first, I'll sue you for damages!"

"Sue and be damned!" yelled Wallace, who saw his wagon boss, Brazos Cobb, arriving. He also saw that he was going to get the aid of twenty seasoned riders.

"Hold, you men, hold!" ordered Brazos, as he came to a stop. "Ten of you waddies get over there and hold back that goddamed Circle 22 herd. The other ten spread out and help herd our cattle in toward the gate."

As the ten sped toward the advancing Villard herd, six of the Villard riders spurred ahead, and there was immediate conflict—shouldering horses, riders swinging with quirts and lariats.

In the vanguard of the Villard men rode Dobie Dick

Donovan. He drew his six-shooter, waved it, fired a shot into the air.

This report added to the noise being made by the riders and the cattle certainly did not add to calming the cattle. Brazos Cobb drew his gun and fired once, well over Donovan's head.

" Put away them guns! " yelled Andy Smith. " Ain't agoin' to stand for no gunfight. Fight all you want to on horseback if you don't use your guns. I'll referee the match if it don't get to be too violent."

The ten riders, all of which were more or less intoxicated, rode so hard, swung so hard, that they gradually forced back the Villard men upon the now frightened and milling herd.

Then, riding like a pygmy on a medium sized buckskin horse, Brazos Cobb charged directly at Dobie Dick Donovan, who, seeing the charge coming, swerved hard, his intent being to shoulder Cobb's horse so hard that it would be knocked off its feet, incidentally pinning its rider underneath and probably killing him.

When it looked as if the two running horses would collide shoulder with shoulder, Cobb kneed his mount hard, swerving it by Donovan's left. As the two horses passed, Cobb drew his gun and stood up in his stirrups and slashed out with the heavy Colt. It clattered against the side of Donovan's reddish head. He slumped, rolled from the saddle, fortunately freeing his feet as he fell.

Either crazy, or discovering he was riderless, Donovan's horse thrust down his head and began to pitch violently.

" Whoops! There's a horse I want! " shouted a drunk cowboy as he loosed his rope.

Travelling at a run he let go his loop and it fell true. His mount slid to a stop so abruptly that Donovan's horse was jerked off its feet. At the corral gate Villard uttered an angry, righteous groan, deploring the fact that one of his best horses had been crippled, possibly killed. By the time Villard had uttered his last words, his horse was on his feet, bucking even more violently.

Another rider charged in, got possession of the rope, jerking it out of the first rider's hand and almost toppling him from the saddle.

"This is my horse, Pete!" shouted the successful rider. "He's exactly the kind of a horse I need. Fine rig on him, too."

Donovan's horse was freed because of preference for personal combat. The two young riders went at it, not on the ground, but from their saddles. Their battle took them away a little and this allowed three men to run in and gather up Donovan about a half-minute before a section of the Circle 22 herd stampeded over the spot where he had lain.

Until now there had been action and noise, now there was chaos because the herds decided to mingle. Heads down and tails waving, they charged each other and certainly mixed in spite of the effort of all the riders to keep them apart. There was bawling, snorting, the rubbing of hairy bodies, the clashing of horns, the yelling and cursing of men. To add, if addition were needed, to this bedlam, a long freight train snorted in from the east and came to a stop with its big locomotive well toward the west end of the yard. In that string of cars were forty empty cattle cars.

The conductor, running toward the station, shouted he had orders to shunt the forty empties on to the shipping pen spur.

"But there's forty on the spur already, Frank," shouted Moreland, the agent. "That spur won't hold eighty."

"Then I'll push 'em on to the sidin'," said the conductor. "I've got orders to drop 'em here."

The conductor was signalling to the engineer when Moreland yelled:

"We've got to keep the siding clear, Frank. I've got orders for you to go into the hole there to let Four pass. She's runnin' on time now and she'll be here in fifteen or twenty minutes. Get off the siding, Frank, and we'll decide what to do with the forty empties. Get a hustle on! Yonder she is, throwing up her smoke at Lone Tree Siding. She'll be here in seven or eight minutes, and somebody'll catch hell if she hasn't got a free track."

Then there was noise as the big locomotive began to snort, and if there was not enough noise, there was the clang of shortening drawbars and the long train slowly got into motion, gathering speed as it backed.

"There are your forty empties, Wallace!" Villard shouted triumphantly. "There in that train. You know tarnation well they're your cars. Sheriff, make peace here so I can get my stock into the pens."

"I'm refereein'!" shouted the sheriff. "I ain't meddlin' unless there's more violence. Can't arrest Brazos Cobb 'cause Dobie was tryin' to ride him down. I hold that Brazos, he acted in self-defence."

"You're sure right I did, Sheriff," Brazos Cobb yelled. "You're just the kind of a sheriff I like. Now we got some cuttin' out to do."

Number Four was coming in with undiminished speed and was laying a long, black plume of coal smoke over her string of mail, baggage, express cars, coaches and sleepers.

Four was whistling for the board, whistling as if telling all the world it had the right-of-way and meant to keep it.

Men, women, children held their breaths, seeing nothing but certain catastrophe.

"Goddam!" a man shouted. "That passenger train's goin' to cut that freight square in two slaunch-wise."

For a minute the human part of the spectacle forgot the cattle, but the cattle did not forget themselves, did not forget that they were mixing, milling, snorting, rubbing, fighting. The human element of that spectacle did not draw a breath until the high-wheeled locomotive of Four shot past a split second after the caboose of the freight had cuddled itself in on the siding, just barely clearing it.

Then the whistle of Number Four reported she was in the clear, and thank God, without a crash!

"And all because of eighty damned empty cattle cars!" swore Fred, the day trick operator. "My God, Wes, there would have been a hundred people killed and maimed if those trains had side-swiped."

Though the cattle and the men trying to part them were making noise enough, a semblance of silence from the human element gathered around three sides of the shipping pens. This evident silence gave the sheriff an opportunity to make a proposition. Tilting back his head and filling his lungs, he yelled:

"There's a way to settle this squabble, Villard and Wallace. Each of you damned fools pick out his best rider and have him pick out a steer of his own brand, and then the first one that pens that steer gets to load all his cattle. That's the way I order it settled. The way those beef are mixed now, you won't get 'em parted out till day after to-morrow."

In front of the depot the freight conductor was angrily trying to explain his orders.

"I know what your orders are, Frank," said Moreland, the agent. "Don't sweat yourself out of your shirt."

"You listen to 'em again, Wes. I got orders to set out forty empty stock cars here and pick up forty loaded ones. Allowed ten minutes to make the shift. To make it worse, I've got to meet with One at Copper Hills."

He pointed dramatically toward the shipping pens, where there still reigned a semblance of quiet.

"Look over there, Wes. From the way it looks to me there ain't a hair off one steer loaded in one car yet, and I was allowed ten minutes to make the shift. What the hell am I to do? I ain't to blame for that mix-up and squabble over who gets one set of cattle cars and who gets the other set. I'll push my forty empties in on that sidin' and get to movin'."

"Now you're clean out of your shirt, Frank," reminded Moreland, who was a fattish, good-natured man. He turned to Fred. " Fred, get headquarters on the wire and see what's to be done in this small dilemma."

" Dilemma, hell," swore the conductor. " It's a mix-up and who's to blame for it? I'm still shiverin' from the way that hoghead on Four damned near side-swiped me. If I'm dragged on the carpet at Winnemucca, by God, I'm goin' to quit! "

" Keep on your shirt, Frank," advised Moreland. " Fred, get division headquarters on the wire. See if you can't get a new order for Frank. He's too valuable a man for the railroad to lose. We can't get along without him."

" Oh, go to hell! " stormed the conductor. " Don't try to josh me. I'm goin' across to the corner and get a drink. Come on, you two shacks, and go with me."

Near the gate to the shipping pens Bill Wallace and George Villard glared at each other, each waiting for the other to speak. Nearby, Jim Villard, lithe, handsome, but loose in his saddle, waited tensely. A little way from him Brazos Cobb crouched in his saddle, his scrawny hands lying tensely on the horn.

" Well, what about it, Dad? " queried Jim Villard. " The offer the sheriff's made seems a fair one to me. Give the word and I'll part out one of our steers and corral it before the best man in the Double W outfit can get started."

" Now, the hell you will! " growled Brazos Cobb. " Kid, before you can even select a steer to part out, I'll have a Double W steer in that pen and the gate shut. Got any money to bet on it? "

" Forty dollars, Brazos! "

" Make it fifty and we'll call it a bet. Have you got fifty? "

" She goes at fifty, Brazos."

Actually seeing Jim Villard for the first time, Bill Wallace said that he'd never before hated a man as he hated this young rider. He hated Jim's father even more. He swung his taunting gaze back to the elder Villard.

"Well, what about it, Villainous? Have you got a quarter-ounce of damned sportin' blood in your Yankee veins? If you have, you'll accept the sheriff's offer."

"By drat, I have, Wallace," shrilled Villard. He then gave part of his wrathful gaze to his son. "Jim, part out one of my cattle and put it in this corral well ahead of any four hoofs and pair of horns belongin' to one of Bill Wallace's steers. Get to movin'! I want to see all of my beef loaded by sundown."

"Just a minute, Villard," snorted the sheriff. "There are a few formalities to be complied with. Line up beside Jim, Brazos, so you can make an even start when I say go."

"I reckon I'll stay right here, Andy," drawled Brazos Cobb after he'd taken a quick look around. "He's as near to that scared Circle 22 steer out there in the sage-brush as I am to the nearest one of Bill Wallace's cattle. Say go when you're ready, Sheriff Smith."

"Then go!" the sheriff barked.

CHAPTER FIVE

THE EDWARDS' blacksmith and wagon shop backed up against the sage at the southern part of town. To west of it was the Edwards' home, surrounded by wind-blown poplar trees. Back of this house, about thirty yards, was a small barn and back of this a corral. In this corral was a buckskin horse which Enid Wallace had ridden over the Two Peaks Mountains from the headquarters of the Double W that day.

Tom Edwards, tall, brawny, red-whiskered, was turning a shoe at his anvil, and thinking he had to shoe Enid's horse all around, when his daughter arrived, breathing hard and flushed of face. Shoving the shoe back into the fire with the tongs, Edwards asked her the cause of all the excitement uptown.

" Why, it's the craziest thing you ever heard of, Dad,"
Lottie said excitedly and paused to catch her breath.
" Yes, it's the funniest. Two fat, clumsy kids could put
up a better fight. Dad, you should have seen it."

" Seen what, Lottie? So far you ain't told me anything."

" But I have! They're having a fight. Just imagine——"

" What am I to imagine about, Lottie? Who's fightin'
and why? "

" But haven't I told you? " she said, giving him a
reproachful look. " It's George Villard and Mr. Bill
Wallace. They went at it hammer and tongs in front of
the depot a while ago."

He now gave her an incredulous stare because in his
mind such rich cattlemen as those two should not be
fighting. It was beneath their dignity. He told her so.
Lottie laughed.

" Dignity! " she said when she could get all her breath.
" That's something, Dad, they didn't have any of.
Here's what I think. I don't believe that either of them
could make a champion pugilist."

At his insistence she gave him details of what she'd seen
and heard. He gave the bellows handle a few pumps,
sat down on the warm anvil and filled his pipe. He was
frowning now.

" Lottie, I don't like the look of this fight," he began.
" No, I don't."

She reminded him that he would have enjoyed it had
he seen it. It was the funniest thing she had ever seen—
two oldish men fighting, and with their fists—wrestling,
swearing, trying to trip and kick each other.

" Daughter, I fail to see anything funny about it," he
said soberly. " There's been bad blood brewin' between
those two outfits for a long time, and now maybe this
fight will bring it to a head. Was Enid Wallace with you
up town, and if she was, what did she do? "

" No, she wasn't, Dad. She's over at the house asleep.
She lay down soon after she rode in a while ago. She was

so tired. She crossed the mountains in seven hours. It seems——"

" Never mind what seems, daughter," he ordered.

After lighting his pipe, he gravely stroked his beard, getting out of it quite a number of coal cinders. He shook his head.

" Lottie, I don't like the looks of these two men fightin'. If it had been a couple of their cowboys, it'd been different. Villard's a strong-headed, stubborn man, and Bill Wallace, he's hot-headed when he gets mad. I don't believe these two will soon forget the fight."

" Neither will I," Lottie said and laughed. " Why, Dad, it was the funniest thing. Honestly, I think I could have licked them both, but they sure went at it. From what I could make out they were fighting over who was to get forty empty cattle cars."

" Well, who got 'em? " Edwards demanded. " If one of 'em got the forty empties, then the other one's goin' to be mad at him for the rest of his life. Lottie, I tell you I don't like this business. They weren't fightin' about Enid, were they ? "

" About Enid? " Lottie said indignantly. " Why should they fight about her? Oh! Do you mean because Enid and Jim Villard are in love? They could have been fighting about that, but I don't think they were, Dad. I think it was all over the empty car business. From what I could gather they were both bringing in their beef herds to load, and each claimed the forty empties."

" Well, if that's all, maybe it's not too serious," said Tom Edwards. " Still when bad blood boils up between two rich cattlemen like that, there's very likely to be some more of it. Were the men drunk? "

Lottie said from what she'd seen, they were not. They were just mad, very mad, so mad they didn't really know how to fight.

" But they sure went at it, Dad," she said and laughed. " Come to think of it, they did fight like clumsy, drunk men, but from what I could catch, I didn't hear anybody say they were drunk."

" No, George Villard seldom drinks," the blacksmith muttered. Again he shook his head, stroked his whiskers.

" But Bill Wallace takes a drink occasionally. He coulda been likkered up a little, though I've never actually seen him drunk."

Remembering that he had a lot of work stacked ahead, he told his daughter he did not want to hear any more about the fight. Hearing what he had heard was shameful enough.

" Yes, because they're rich cattlemen," she said sarcastically. " If they'd been a couple of ordinary cowboys, you wouldn't have given it a second thought, Dad. I'll go tell Mother about it. She'll see the funny side of it."

Though Mrs. Edwards said she wished she could have seen the fight, she added that she saw nothing funny about it. In her opinion it was disgraceful, such men as Villard and Wallace fighting there in front of the depot. It was a blot upon the fair name of the sagebrush country, a disgrace, a shame! They were just old fools!

" It's mighty lucky Enid was sleeping sound," she said and sighed. " It'd been awful on that girl if she'd seen her father fightin' Villard, and him maybe runnin' on close to sixty years old, though I've heard he does claim to be only about fifty-four. Is Jim Villard in town, Lottie? "

Shaking her auburn head, Lottie said she did not know because the Villard herd had not yet arrived. It was down where the bridge crossed the river, and the Wallace herd was coming in from the west. There was bound to be more trouble, as nearly two thousand cattle couldn't be put in forty cars.

" Well, let 'em thrash out their own troubles," Mrs. Edwards declared. " Both men are good customers of your father's at times. Lottie, don't you take sides."

Lottie agreed with a nod, but what she thought was something entirely different. Why shouldn't she take sides? Enid was her most intimate girl friend, and there wasn't a rider on the Circle 22 payroll, including Jim Villard himself, that she would accept if he were handed to her on a silver platter with about a thousand dollars as trimmings.

" I'm awful afraid, Lottie, that this will bust up the love affair between Enid and Jim Vallard," Lottie's mother said and sighed. She was a sighing woman. " They would have made such a handsome couple, too."

" It won't bust it up, Mother," said Lottie. " They think too much of each other. I've seen them making love, and they do a good job of it, and I'm sure if it wasn't for Enid, I could fall in love with Jim, even if he is a Villard, he's that handsome and manly."

" And what's the matter with being a Villard? " Mrs. Edwards demanded. " George Villard is just as rich as Bill Wallace is, and he's as good a man, too. No, he ain't. He's a down-east Republican, and your Pa, he always votes a Democrat ticket. That'd make a little difference, but just the same, Lottie, do you know whether Villard and Wallace had guns on 'em? "

" If they did, they weren't using them," Lottie said and laughed. " But, my gosh, Mother, each of 'em was trying to use all the weapons nature had given him. Listen to the noise over there toward the shipping pens. The herds must be arriving. What do you think about it, should I awake Enid? "

" And see her father shame her? " Mrs. Edwards snapped, and then sighed. " I'm for lettin' the girl sleep, she's that tired, and what she don't see won't hurt her. Just let her be, Lottie. I took a look at her a little while ago and she's sleepin' so sound and nice in there in the front room on the couch, layin' flat on her back with her lips parted a little. She's an awful pretty girl, ain't she? "

" Yes, she really is," Lottie said soulfully, a little enviously, " with her clear complexion and her grey eyes and her long black hair."

" And don't forget her shape, Lottie. She's a mighty

shapely girl, even a little more shapely than you are, and you're plenty shapely. Lottie, I do wish you'd wear looser dresses so the men wouldn't look at you so much."

"Oh, let 'em look!" Lottie said and laughed. "I can't help it if I'm built the way I am. Of course, if I ate less I might shrink myself down to my dresses, but eating is such fun. I'll take a peek at Enid."

During the next hour and thirty minutes, Lottie Edwards looked in on her sleeping friend fifteen times, each time saying silently:

"Dammit, why doesn't she wake up? There's so much unusual happening up there I wanted to see it, and it wouldn't be fair for me to go without taking her. I got a notion to——"

Then Lottie's will melted under the heat of eagerness and curiosity. She shouted:

"Enid, wake up! You don't know what you're missing! Wake up, Enid!"

Enid's eyes slowly opened. She yawned, stretched. She was about to close her long-lashed lids again when Lottie grabbed her by the shoulders and shook her violently.

"Wake up, Enid! I want to tell you about the fight your father and Villainous Villard had. It was the funniest thing. Enid, I'll roll you off that couch and sit on you if you go back to sleep, and I'll tickle you and I'll pinch you where you wouldn't let a man pinch you. Are you going to wake up? It was the funniest fight—I mean the one your father and Villard had."

That penetrated Enid's conscience so deeply and abruptly that she sat up. She demanded to be told whether anybody had been killed.

"No, neither of those two old fools!" Lottie said and laughed. "But it was the funniest thing, Enid. They couldn't fight any better than a couple of fat kids, but they were sure going at it. Wake up so I can tell you all about it."

"Darn it, I'm awake, Lottie. You can see that," Enid cried out. "What's all that noise?"

"All that noise? Why, the two herds are mixed, and cowboys are ridin' and fightin' and shootin'. How do I know? I climbed a tree a while ago so I could see. It's the awfullest mix up over towards the shipping pens, and I was just dying to go and be there, but Enid, I just couldn't go and leave you. I'm not sure, but I think I saw Jim Villard."

"You saw Jim! Are you sure of that?" Enid cried out. "Here, Lottie, you put on my boots while I fix up my hair. If there's going to be more trouble, Jim Villard must not be killed."

"I don't believe he's going to be killed," Lottie panted. "From all that noise everybody's still alive, even about two thousand cattle. Darn it, hold out your foot! Enid, do you know you've been asleep for more than two hours?"

"And why the devil didn't you wake me two hours ago?" Enid demanded, frantically trying to wind a long braid about the crown of her small head. "Lottie, why on earth did you let me sleep with all this happening? I'll be ready in five minutes, but I've just got to go out to the back yard first."

"So have I," Lottie giggled. "My father says that this fight between your father and Villard may result in a range war."

"I don't care if it does," Enid declared, as she stood up and pushed her small feet into her boots. "All I care about is that Jim doesn't get hurt, but if there is a range war, it won't make any difference between him and me. He's told me that already. Come on, let's go!"

Knowing well that there was no saying where half wild, frightened cattle would decide to go, the crowd broke away from the shipping pens, moved back in a straggling line to eastward. Sheriff Andy Smith, exhorting and swearing, managed to get down the fence roosters, and these he herded toward the rest of the crowd.

"Get off the tops of those empty cars, boys!" the

sheriff yelled. "Give these cuttin' horses a fair show. Either climb down or lay down."

The boys flattened on the catwalks of the slightly sloping roofs, but not one of them descended.

"Got five dollars that says Jim Villard pens his steer first!" a man yelled. "He's got the best damned cuttin' horse in Nevada."

"Your money is took!" another man shouted. "Best cuttin' horse, hell! That buckskin Brazos Cobb's ridin' could cut a single whisker out of the devil's beard and never miss a jump. I've got another five that says Brazos puts his steer in the corral first."

"You're took, Jackson!"

"I got ten cents that says neither steer's penned," said a boy on top of the car directly in front of the loading chute. "Who wants to cover my money?"

"I'll bet you ten marbles and three fish-hooks and a ball of string," another boy said. "I ain't got ten cents in money."

There was suspense, eagerness, actual holding of breath, but certainly not silence. Brazos Cobb and Jim Villard cut out their respective steers at the same moment, turned them. After that their cow horses knew what to do, and without more than knee guiding.

"Get in there, you striped, black son-of-a-bitch!" Brazos Cobb yelled. "Don't let him double back, Buck."

"Right in that gate yonder," Jim Villard told his horse. "Watch him, there's no tellin' what he'll do, he's as crazy as a loon!"

Straight toward the open gate the steers charged with the riders close behind, as if at last, both cattle were content to go anywhere and gain peace, if only for a minute.

"By God, Jim's goin' to put his critter in first!" a man yelled. "He's doin' the best work of cuttin' if somethin' don't happen."

Then something did happen! Just when it looked as though the Circle 22 steer was going to shoot straight through the open gate, through the straggled crowd broke two young women at their best run—one in whitish buckskin, the other in crimson wool. They did not stop and mix with the crowd, but continued to run. They were holding hands, but that left them two hands free to wave. There was plenty of skirt fluttering, particularly fluttering of the red skirt, which was ankle length.

"For God's sake, get back there, girls!" the sheriff shouted. "Let this be fair play. Come back, come back!"

Sight of that red dress was too much for the Circle 22 steer. It slid to a stop, seemed to turn on an area no larger than a dinner plate. With head down and tail waving it shot back along the right side of Jim Villard's horse, and the Double W steer went like a tail-waving thunderbolt straight through the opening into the shipping pens.

Brazos Cobb uttered a shrill, triumphant war whoop, sprang from the saddle, grabbed the gate and dragged it shut. "And now who wins?" Brazos challenged, waving his hat. "Who's got the best cuttin' horse in Nevada? Me, what's more, I know how to ride it! Where's Bill Wallace? Bill! Begin loadin' your beef!"

"Begin loadin' my beef hell, Brazos," Wallace shouted as he hurried out of the crowd. "Hell, man, don't you see there's about a thousand more of them to be cut out yet. Of all the messes I ever saw, and it's all Villard's fault, too. Look at them herds, ain't they mixed? It'll take us till midnight to get 'em cut out. Get your men to work, Brazos, get 'em to work. We can't cut cattle after dark!"

Brazos jumped to his saddle and sped away, to get every possible man to work, and Bill Wallace stopped, waved his hands, swore as he saw one lonely, Double W steer in the corral and nearly a thousand more to be put there, and into the cars.

Villainous Villard, after seeing the Double W win, beheld one thing—a fool girl in a crimson dress. Stamping the ground, waving his arms, Villard was bearing down

on her when he discovered that there was another girl—
a girl in whitish buckskin.

"Damn you, Enid Wallace!" he yelled, as he stormed
at her. "No wonder I don't want my boy to marry you,
you ain't got sense enough to carry swill to a hog. Get
away from here, young woman, before I lose my patience
and become violent. Don't you see you caused me to
lose hundreds of dollars, not to mention losin' my pride
by lettin' Bill Wallace pen his steer first!"

Just when it looked as though Villard was going to lay
violent hands upon Enid Wallace, a hurriedly-thrown
riata flew out, its loop settling truly over Villard's shoulders, as the sorrel horse that had missed penning its steer
first settled back and Jim Villard threw a dally around
the horn. The next moment his enraged father was
sprawling in the dust, flat on his back and half-stunned
for a moment, at the end of which, he got savagely to his
feet and whirled.

"Who in tarnation roped me without my consent?"
he shouted. "Show me the colour of that man's eyes and
I'll kill him!"

"Sure, go ahead and kill him! Go ahead and kill
him!" chortled Bill Wallace. "Go ahead and kill your
own flesh and blood, Villard, it's just like you, you
damned cattle stealin' skunk! That there's my daughter,
and if you lay a hand on her, Villard, I'll kill you so dead
you won't skin. Don't you lay a hand on that girl!
That goes for you, too, Jim Villard! You're a Villard!
Don't you even look at her!"

But Jim Villard, barely hearing Enid's irate father, was
out of his saddle and springing towards the buckskin clad
girl who was tottering towards him. They collided, em-
braced as if they were the only two people in this vast,
grey sagebrush country.

There would have come a complete silence but for the
bawling and running of cattle and the yelling and swearing of riders, and the hissing of steam from the overloaded
safety valve of the freight locomotive.

" Oh, my God, my God," groaned Frank, the conductor of the freight. " I got my new orders and they tell me to wait here until Wallace loads his cattle and to haul 'em out, and there's one lone steer in the corral, and a young man and a young woman makin' love, and two thousand cattle millin' yonder in the sagebrush. I'll be here next Christmas! "

" Do the best you can, Frank," encouraged Moreland, the agent. " That's all you can do."

" And I'm tellin' you, Wallace," threatened Villard, " that if you ship one of my cattle, even by mistake, I'll have the law on you! Don't forget that! "

" And let me tell you this, you villainous old varmint! " snorted Wallace. " If you ship one of my cattle by mistake, I'll shoot you, the hell with the law! Wait, I want to tell you somethin' else, and here it is with the bark on it. If you ever let that worthless boy of yours lay hands on my daughter again, I'll cut our your heart! Do you savvy that? "

" Yes, I understand that, you old disgraceful varmint," shrilled Villard. " Now, listen to me. If you ever let that worthless girl of yours wrap her arms around my boy's neck again like she's done here in public, and disgraced me and my son, I'll set my best men on your whole outfit and run you and your whole outfit clean out of the State of Nevada! Is that plain enough, or do I have to make it plainer? "

" That's plain enough, Villard," said Bill Wallace with a mirthless chuckle. He swung hard and landed, and the next moment the owner of the Circle 22 was hitting the dust full length.

Men pulled them apart before they could actually begin to fight. It was Jim Villard himself who shouted:

" Go down there towards the river, you two old badgers, if you want to fight it out. It seems to me that our business here is to part out cattle and load them as fast as we can. Don't you think so, Enid? "

She could only nod, but that was affirmative enough

for him, especially as she clung to him, making it extremely difficult for him to break away and regain his saddle.

"I'll have to be goin' now, honey, there's plenty of work for me to do."

"Yes, you go, Jim. You'll find me at the Edwards' home when you are through—no matter how late you finish. Look at our fathers!"

"Let 'em fight it out!" declared Jim Villard. "Neither of them know how to handle a gun so they can't do much harm."

But Villard and Wallace had temporarily forgotten their feud. Both were yelling for somebody to get the locomotive in on the spur so it could begin spotting cars at the chute and Wallace was yelling for somebody to load that lone steer.

"It's a nice quite afternoon, ain't it?" inquired Hitchcock, owner of the Empire Hotel.

"Oh, it is indeed," agreed Dave Berry, who owned and operated the Club Saloon. "It'll take 'em till to-morrow night to part out those cattle and load them. What do you say to us goin' and havin' a couple of drinks, Hitchcock?"

CHAPTER SIX

THE LOCOMOTIVE shoved back the string of empties until the door of the foremost car was opposite the loading chute. Big Sage had seen many cattle loaded, but never before had it witnessed the mixing of two sizeable herds with about forty riders trying to part each individual brand. For a time it looked as though there was nobody directing the parting, then Jim Villard said:

"As the Double W stuff is to be loaded first, we'll let Brazos Cobb be boss. Seems to me that'll be fair. Dad,

I'm sure Mr. Wallace won't try to steal any of your cattle."

"Don't you be tellin' me what's what, Jim," his father bristled. "You don't know that old reprobate as well as I do. Once a steer with my brand gets into that shippin' pen, that'll be the last I'll ever see of it."

"But dammit, Villard," the sheriff swore. "You know as well as I do that ain't true. When this stuff gets to the stockyards in San Francisco, every brand will be examined, and you'll get your money if any of your brand's in there. Quit bein' a damned old fool."

"And you quit meddlin' with my business," Villard retorted. "I'm able to take care of my own business, Sheriff Smith, and you know it. I'm goin' to stay right here close to the gate and see that none of my brand gets in there."

"And I'm goin' to stay right here close to the gate and see that I don't get any of his damned stuff in with mine!" Wallace cursed. "I wouldn't disgrace my beef by havin' a sample of his in with it. Lock him up, Andy!"

"Well, if I do," said the sheriff, "I'll lock you up with him. Have you two old cattlemen lost all your brains? Now, if you insist standin' one on each side of the gate, you know they can't pen a single beef. Aside from bein' wild, these cattle are all scared now and plenty excited. I don't want to have to use force on you two, but, by gosh, it seems to me you should get a little sense. If you must quarrel or fight, go over there on the other side of the tracks and fight it out."

"Won't do it!" Villard growled. "I'm goin' to stay right here! Goin' to see that none of my stuff gets penned with his."

"And by God, Villard, I'm going to stay right here and see that none of your ornery stuff gets in with mine!" cursed Wallace.

The sheriff said that he'd stay and see that nothing with Villard's brand on it got into the corral, but this

argument failed. Villard declared that they were his
cattle and he'd stay and see they were not stolen.

"Why, you damned old cattle thief!" cursed Wallace.
"You know you got your start with your big herd by
stealin' it! Everybody in the country knows that, and
now you're scared of me shippin' one of your beef by
mistake. I wouldn't ship even the dry hide of one of your
beef, Villard, and you know it. I'll admit that now and
then one of my riders puts my brand on a slick-ear, and
I'm not ashamed of it, but you're so damned righteous
you think all the world's tryin' to rob you. If you'da
had any sense you'da held your herd back and not mixed
it all up with mine, and if I had any sense I'da licked hell
out of you over there at the depot instead of quittin'!"

"Quittin'!" stormed Villard. "You quit because I
was about to lick you. I'm sorry now I didn't do it."

"And I'll lock you both up if you don't quit quarrellin' with each other," the sheriff promised.

This had no effect, however, and just when it looked
as if the two wealthy ranchers were going into battle
again, Enid and Lottie ran forward, Enid half-dragging
the reluctant Miss Edwards.

"I think I can do something with my father, Lottie.
He and Mr. Villard aren't doing a bit of good here and
they know it, but they're both as bull-headed as a couple
of old roan Durham bulls."

"Ho, ho, ho," cursed Villard as he saw the girls.
"There you are, young filly, with that red dress on—get
out of here. Don't you see we're tryin' to pen cattle?
If you want to use that red dress for anything, go down to
Mexico and use it in a bull-fight."

He turned his venom then upon Enid, ordering her to
get out of his sight, never to let him set eyes on her again
She was the young hussy that had all but ruined his son.

"Your son," cursed Wallace. "Hell! Villard, he was
ruined from the day he was born and here's why. It's
because he has your blood in him. Let those girls stay
and hear if they want to, and if you don't want 'em to

stay, Villard, let's get to work and see who's boss, you or me."

Villard and Wallace were rushing at each other, snarling and grappling when the sheriff sprang between them. With out-thrust of both hands, he shoved them back. He used thumb and forefinger to get a hold of Villard's right ear, and before Wallace could see what was happening to his hated enemy, his left ear was gripped by the sheriff's other thumb and forefinger. The wealthy cattlemen started to pitch and sidle like as many colts feeling the saddle for the first time, but to no avail because the more they struggled to free themselves, the more intense was the pain.

The sheriff called for help and got plenty of it.

" Here, men," Sheriff Smith ordered, " get the handcuffs on them. I'm plumb weary of this damned foolishness. I'll lock these two old longhorn bulls up and maybe at least some of those cattle can be loaded."

" By drat, you don't lock me up in any of your calibooses! " cursed Villard. " If you even take me in that direction—even put handcuffs on me, I'll have the law on you, Smith! I'll sue you for such damages that you'll never get money enough to pay me."

" Oh, the hell you will? " demanded the sheriff. " I'll see about that."

" Lock him up! Lock him up! " chortled Wallace. " That's the only way to put any sense in his head. Lock him up and keep him locked up for a week, Andy."

" Yes, and while I'm lockin' him up," growled the sheriff, " I'll lock you up too, Bill. Each of you are doin' more harm than good, and both of you know it, but neither of you have got the sense enough to admit it."

" Enid, are you going to stand by and see your father locked up? " Lottie said, trying this as a test. " That'll be a disgrace, won't it? "

" Yes, let him be locked up," Enid retorted. " As for disgrace, he's disgracin' us now by acting like he is. Besides——"

" Yes, besides what, honey? "

" I'm willin' to see my father locked up just to see Villard locked up. Why, he's even meaner than I thought he was, but——"

" But what, honey? "

" But, he isn't making any bigger a fool of himself than my father is."

With the noisy crowd acting as convoy, the sheriff and his prisoners were nearing the board-fence that surrounded the spare ground of the Empire Hotel when a man shouted :

" Hey, Sheriff Smith, why not handcuff 'em to a couple of fence posts so they can't get at each other, but they can paw dirt and beller like the fool old bulls they are? If you take 'em all the way to your jail, you'll miss so much of the show. Here, these two fence posts will do, they're only about fifteen feet apart."

Within about a minute the wealthy owner of the Double W and the wealthy owner of the Circle 22 were shackled to two fence posts that had originally been railroad ties.

" Now paw the dirt and beller! " drawled the man that had suggested this means of imprisonment.

After having been knocked from his saddle by a blow from Brazos Cobb's sixshooter, Dobie Dick Donovan had been carried to a point near the shipping pen and laid upon the ground. His horse had been left nearby, reins down. Now, coming back to consciousness but still dazed, the Circle 22 wagon boss struggled to his feet, and for several minutes supported himself by clutching the boards of the shipping corral.

At first he was conscious only of noise, but gradually knowledge of what was going on drilled its way into his paining head. He managed to get to his horse. He tested the cinch and dragged himself into the saddle.

Seeing that his foreman was able to ride, Villard lifted his voice to its extreme pitch yelling for Donovan to come, and free him from this iniquitious disgrace, which was made worse by the proximity of the Double W owner.

Donovan came at a slow trot, each thud of a hoof on the ground seeming to half jar the top of his head off. He reined up, but instead of being angry, he grinned in a silly fashion.

" Well, now, if they ain't snubbed up my boss to a post," he chuckled. " Villard, what have you been doin' while I was down an out? "

" Doin'? I been tryin' to protect my rights, Dobie! Free me from this fence post. Never before in all my years have I suffered such humiliation and disgrace. Get me free from here, Donovan. Put your rope on this post and pull this tarnation fence down. Get me free any way way you can."

" There, Dobie Dick," Wallace shouted, " you see a sample of the humiliation I have to suffer by bein' so damned near a varmint like him. If you'll sniff the air you'll discover he smells like a polecat."

" By drat, Wallace, I've endured enough of that! " Villard shouted as he glared at his hated enemy. " I'll tolerate no more of it."

The sheriff nearby was prepared to interfere in case the Circle 22 wagon boss attempted to free Villard. He said: " Dobie, they're my prisoners and I'm goin' to keep 'em right here until those cattle are loaded. If you try to meddle, I'll tie you up to another fence post."

" Oh, I'm not goin' to meddle, Andy," Donovan said, his voice still shaky. " There's too many cattle to be separated out for me to monkey with him. Seems to me you've got him in a good place, where he can make plenty of noise and breathe in plenty of fresh air and do plenty of preachin'. I've got work to do."

With that, Donovan turned his horse and trotted away toward where Brazos Cobb and four other riders were nursing a small bunch of cattle toward the gate of the shipping pens.

Fright and anger now struck deep into the sheriff's

brain and heart. There was going to be shooting trouble
and he didn't even have a horse to ride in and stop it.
He yelled for somebody to bring him a horse, for Donovan
to stop, to turn and come back.

"Enid, don't you think we'd better go home?"
Lottie Edwards begged. "We don't seem to be doing
any good here. I'm sure the sheriff will let your father
go soon."

"The sheriff won't let him loose soon!" Smith
growled. "Those riders will be lucky if they get those
Double W steers loaded by dark, and I'm goin' to hold
these two old fools here and do what I can toward helpin'
out. Yes, you girls best go on home, as I'm quite sure
you aren't doin' any good."

"Doin' any good! Doin' any good!" Villard yelled.
"If it hadn't been for that filly there with the red dress
on, I'd be loadin' my beef now instead of losin' out to old
Wallace here. Make 'em go home, Smith. They make
me madder and madder every time I look at 'em."

Giving Villard a look, which in the intensity of its
contempt and fury should have burned off the fence post
to which the owner of the Circle 22 was shackled, Enid
turned back to her girl friend and said with forced mix-
ture of resignation and sweetness:

"Yes, Lottie, we'll go now. We really can't do any
good here and, besides, we can help your mother get
supper."

They marched sedately away, and as they went old
Nora Marr, who had been an occupant of Big Sage since
its first house was built, said loudly and shrilly:

"All this here racket, it's sure buildin' up a fine,
lovable atmosphere for Enid and Jim Villard to live in
once they get married. Yes, folks, their married life will
be as smooth and tranquil as the bottom of a rocky gulch
infested by rattlesnakes and cactus."

Seeing Brazos Cobb circle wide of the small bunch of
cattle that were being, with much difficulty, driven toward the shipping pens, Sheriff Smith set off at a lope,

frightened and shamed by his oversight in permitting this shooting trouble. Hell, of course, there was going to be shooting trouble because Brazos Cobb was riding straight toward Dobie Dick Donovan, and Dobie Dick was veering neither to right nor left, and certainly not stopping and turning back.

"Well, how about it, Donovan?" Cobb sneered as they stopped their horses with heads almost rubbing. "Are you of a mind to finish up that little quarrel we had a while ago? I can take about a minute off to kill you."

"No, I'm not huntin' up trouble with you right now, Brazos," Donovan said without the least show of concession. "There's too damned much work to do for us to go to fightin' it out at the present minute. You scrawny little Texas son-of-a-bitch, have you ever stopped to think that me and you have about all the cattle savvy there is in this crazy outfit? Have you ever stopped to think of that?"

"Well, yes, I've got some cattle savvy, and you've got a little less, Donovan," said Cobb, making a small concession. "What's your big idea, you long, lanky, Irish bastard? Is it as how that me and you should superintend the partin' out of these cattle in order it'll be done proper? Is it somethin' like that?"

"It's along those lines, Cobb," conceded the Circle 22 wagon boss, his bloodshot eyes glaring malevolently. "I ain't suggestin', though, that our quarrel be postponed indefinite. What you say we declare a truce of a day or two or maybe three in order we can get these goddamned cattle shipped in their proper cars? As likely you know by this time I ain't a man to forget my personal troubles with you. How about you, Brazos?"

"I'm a good rememberin' man, Dobie," said Brazos, drawing up an end of his wide mouth. "I think this here plan's the best for the present, because if we leave it to Wallace and Villard, they won't fill a car with beef in four weeks, they're that crazy mad at each other. My ears are open to any suggestion you've got."

" I suggest we pull in about four or five of our men to help with the loadin', Brazos, and order those no-account town riders to spread out and keep the cattle from scatterin' to the four winds of hell."

Brazos was about to declare there was nothing yet to be loaded, then he saw one Double W steer and then another and then another shoot through the open gate into the shipping pens until the entire small bunch was in.

" Twenty-five in that bunch, boys! " Brazos yelled happily. " Shut the gate and load 'em and by the time you get 'em in a car and another car's spotted, Dobie and me and our men'll have another bunch here. Come on, Donovan, let's me and you go and show those goddamned no-account riders how to part out cattle. Hey, you, Tommy Jones, scatter yourself out and find the rest of your town would-be buckaroos and tell 'em to ride the fringes of this herd to keep 'em from scatterin' all to hell."

After that, though the sun sank swiftly toward the flat saddle that connected the two rounded peaks, everything worked with a celerity, which the onlookers had not expected. Bunch after bunch were swiftly run into the shipping pens. Car after car was loaded. Time and again the locomotive snorted, butted up another empty car. Then as the sun dropped out of sight and twilight began to enfold the grey land and for a time make it beautiful, the last car was loaded, its door was closed, bolted and the locomotive, labouring with a load of forty filled cars, began to snort its way toward the end of the spur, and a few minutes later was backing in on the siding to connect up with the rest of the regular freight and then uncouple and push forty more empties in on to the shipping pen spur.

Brazos Cobb, weary enough to drop from his saddle, trotted swiftly toward where his boss and Villard were still shackled to the two fence posts. Brazos didn't have to stop his weary horse, it stopped of its own accord.

" Well, you done good work, Brazos," Wallace conceded. " Load all my beef? "

" No, we had to send 'em out forty short, Bill," Cobb explained. " Them forty's mixed in with the Circle 22 stuff. We'll part 'em out in the morning unless that low-down polecat there, chained to the other post, wants to let 'em be shipped with his cattle and settlement be made later."

" No, by drat, by drat! " shrilled Villard. " I agreed on no such proposition as that. Here's why. I won't contaminate my good beef by allowin' any scrub stuff, like Wallace raises, to be shipped with mine. That's my order! "

" Which I plumb accept," agreed Dobie Dick Donovan, who had ridden up. " If you can cool down your mad a little, Villard, here's somethin' I'd like to remind you of. You've got quite a good bunch of beef out there in the sagebrush for to-night. How about orderin' up a couple loads of hay from the livery stable in town so they'll have somethin' besides sagebrush to eat on durin' the night? That'll keep 'em from too much shrinkage, and about daylight in the mornin', we'll drive 'em down to the river to water. Want me to see about the hay? "

" I'll personally see about the hay, Donovan," Villard corrected angrily.

" But you're hitched up, Villard," a man reminded with forced soberness. " I ain't seen the sheriff make any move yet to unhitch you two."

" I'll turn 'em loose," said the sheriff, fumbling in his overalls' pocket for his handcuff keys. " I'll let 'em loose on this condition—that they mustn't try to sleep in the same bed to-night."

" Oh, I'll sleep in the same bed with the damned varmint," growled Bill Wallace. " It'd give me a good chance to cut his throat. You're plumb safe in turnin' me loose, Andy."

" And I," Villard declared with high and hot dignity,

"am quite comfortable where I am, if you take that old reprobate out of my sight."

The sheriff said he was sorry to disoblige Villard, but he was going to turn both of them loose, and shoot the pair of them if they even began a quarrel.

"All right, all right," growled Villard. "You're the law here, Smith, have it your own way."

"And I'm warnin' you, Villainous Villard," promised Wallace, determined to have the last word, "I'm goin' to blind you with tobacco juice if you so much as scowl at me. Turn him loose, Andy, so he can get a good start!"

CHAPTER SEVEN

IN EXTREMELY high dudgeon, Villard was marching toward the Astor House, where he stayed when he was in Big Sage, when he was passed by three galloping volunteer riders. They slid their horses to a stop when they recognised the owner of the Circle 22.

"Hey, Villainous," they demanded. "Come likker up with us! We sure made a pronto job of pennin' them cattle. Come along."

He ignored this by seeming not to see them, and by marching on. He was madder now, even sorrier for himself. The three dusty and sweat-streaked riders kept pace with him.

"Hey, Mr. Villard," one of them said. "Seems to me you owe me ten dollars. Ten'll come in mighty handy. Won't it to you boys, too?"

Each of the other riders said he could find room for ten dollars in his pocket, and would appreciate it immediately. That stopped Villard in his tracks.

"I owe you men nothing!" he said irately. "I made no such promise. Take your complaint to Wallace. He's a man of no brains."

"That's why we stopped and talked to you, Villainous. You've got a lot of brains—course, Bill Wallace is crazy. He ain't a smart rancher like you are, Villainous."

Now Villard was even madder, more insulted, more hurt. In his own opinion he was not a mean man, he was merely a purposeful, careful, far-seeing gentleman of the range country, who demanded everything that belonged to him and just a little more.

Seeing Wallace shuffling along behind, the cowboys turned their horses, and stopped him just as three more of their fellows arrived from the herd which Brazos Cobb and Dobie Dick Donovan were putting under night guard.

Six demands of ten dollars each were immediately made upon Wallace, who, not having that much money in his pocket, tried making these half-dozen riders believe that their money was good, that they'd be paid to-morrow.

"Tell you what we'll do, Mr. Wallace," declared Tommy Jones, who'd declared himself spokesman. "Dig up five dollars apiece and we'll call it square. 'Course, you bein' a thorough cattleman know that each of us earned at least fifty dollars. Why, that was the damndest mix-up of cattle we ever run across. Most rode my horse to death. Of course, if my horse dies, I'll expect you to buy me another one."

"Just keep on expectin' it," Wallace ordered and tried to get past, but in vain. Then he discovered that he had thirty dollars in his pocket and that he could make thirty dollars by settling now. "Why, yes, boys I reckon you did ride pretty hard cuttin' out them goddamned Villard cattle. Wait'll I see whether I can make the proper change. Yep! Here it is. Five dollars apiece you say? Climb out of your saddles and take your money because I'm too tired to reach it up to you."

By the time this settlement had been made, four more volunteer riders arrived, and on seeing what was occurring, demanded their cash.

"At a fifty per cent discount, boys," Tommy Jones said grandly. "That's the way we settled. You'd best take what you can get as this old son-of-a-bitch may not be very good pay. That's why us hombres settled for five apiece."

"What's that! What's that?" exploded Wallace who had been trying to determine with his fingers how much more money he had left in his pocket. "Show me the colour of the man's eyes that says I don't pay my bills and I'll kill the son-of-a-bitch. I'm on the warpath anyway, to-day. Who made that remark about me not bein' too honest?"

"Oh, Villainous Villard made it," said Johnny Granger soberly. "We're just givin' it to you second-hand, Mr. Wallace. Boys, didn't we all hear Mr. Villard say that Mr. Wallace seldom pays his bills?"

"Yes, that's plumb right, Johnny," agreed the other five, including Jones. "Them ain't the exact words Villard used but we're giving you his meaning all right."

"Then I'm goin' to kill Villard!" Wallace snorted. "Him talkin' that way about me when the old son-of-a bitch will argue for five hours to save five cents! You four boys, I'm awfully sorry, but I ain't got twenty left. Is my credit good?"

"Well, Villainous Villard says it ain't!" Johnny Granger said as if reluctant. "I leave it to a vote of the other boys to see what we do."

The other boys unanimously declared, but as though very reluctant to make this statement, that they wouldn't trust Bill Wallace as far as they could throw a big bull uphill by the tail.

"Then, by God, follow me over to Dodge Brothers' store and I'll settle up with you!" Wallace said with an indignant snort. "Round up the rest of your fool partners and I'll pay them off, too. Come along! In case you don't know it, the store's right across the street yonder."

"We know where it is, Mr. Wallace," Johnny Granger said. "We buy cigarette tobacco there."

E

In the big general store Wallace demanded of Lou Dodge to be told whether his credit was good for twenty dollars as four young highwaymen were standing him up for twenty.

"Why, yes, Bill, I guess we can let you have that much money," said Lou, who was tall and lanky and homely. "That is if you'll give us a chattel mortgage on a two-year old steer."

"Chattel mortgage, hell!" Wallace swore. "I won't give you nothing. Say, tell me this, did my chuckwagon load here this afternoon?"

"Yes, it did," Lou Dodge said soberly. "Porky was in here about the middle of the afternoon and loaded up about three hundred dollars' worth of grub which I had to charge to your account. I guess we can run the risk of lettin' you have another twenty."

"Then dammit, do it, Lou!" Wallace ordered.

He soon settled with the four riders, though indignantly. He realized that he had made fifty dollars, though he did not forget there was another ten to be paid off. Such payment as this was an outrage because he could hire an ordinary range cowboy to work for forty a month.

Leaving their horses tied at the Dodge Brothers' hitchrail, the ten cowboys trooped across the dusty side street, on their way to the saloon, but got no farther than half way when Johnny Granger called a halt. There, he almost oratorically pointed out what their financial condition would be to-morrow morning—yes, even within a few hours. As a self-respecting, hard-working cowboy, he couldn't stay in Big Sage flat broke.

"That's right, Johnny," Tommy Jones agreed. "Here's how I feel when I'm flat broke, with a belly full of whisky. I feel like a woman who has just had a baby—all flattened out. Don't you fellows feel the same way when you're flat broke and half a skin full of whisky?"

In a few argumentative minutes they agreed that they would not let the sun of to-morrow rise on them and see them in a penniless condition. No, sir, they'd hold up somebody first.

"Here's what we'll do, boys," declared Jones. "We'll just lay for old Villainous Villard, and the first time he shows his nose outdoors, we'll rob him. Here's why it won't be no crime to rob that old bastard. Wait'll I make and light a cigarette."

"Why won't it be no crime to rob old Villard?" demanded Gimpy, who was just a little afraid of landing in jail. "Robbin' him will be the same as robbin' anybody else, won't it?"

"No, it won't. Here's why," said Jones, with the gravity of a long and lanky dust-covered judge. "Let's say that Villard owes us five apiece. We worked just as hard partin' out his beef as we did partin' out Wallace's beef, and Wallace trundled up right off. Takin' five apiece away from old Villard won't be robbery, it'll be the extraction of honest deserts."

"Hold on, you mavericks," shouted Johnny Granger. "Yonder's the Club Saloon. Let's hightail into it and get a couple of drinks and then find the Chinaman. I'm as hungry as hell!"

After about five minutes of argument, that included threats upon his life and the promise of three free drinks of whisky, the nine convinced Gimpy that he should go get the horses and take them to the combined livery stable and feed corral, and leave them there, where they could eat grain.

"By gosh, boys, I'll do it," agreed Gimpy, who didn't have more than three-quarters of the sense God Almighty had meant him to have. "I'll see you over at the Club, and damn you, don't you drink my three drinks, either."

"Get goin', Gimp," said Jones. "If you don't find us at the Club, you'll find us at the Chinaman's."

"Gimp, you're just the man I want to see," said Lou Dodge. "What do you want? It'll be on the house if it don't cost more'n a dollar."

"What do I want, Lou?" Gimp said and snickered. "Let me see. Give me a five-cent sack of Durham and throw in a pack of papers, and we'll call it square."

"It's a deal, Gimpy. Here you are. I'll throw in two packs of papers—no, I'll make it two sacks of Durham, too."

The squat, hatchet-faced, crooked-nosed cowboy grabbed his prizes and started to hurry out, but Lou Dodge stopped him with:

"Come back, Gimp. We haven't started to talk business."

"Talk business? Lou, I don't know a damned thing about business. I'm just a fool cowboy with no sense."

"Just the man I want, then," Lou Dodge reassured. "Come on, let's go out in front where we won't be bothered. This is mighty important. If you can't make a fortune out of it, Gimp, you can make fame. Want to be famous?"

"I don't know! I never was famous. All right, I'll go ahead and listen, but I ain't got time to spare."

They went out to the pitted boardwalk, beyond which ten hungry horses stood restlessly and shook their bridles. One whickered, then another, then another until it seemed ten dozen had whickered.

"Lou, them horses are hungry. I got to take 'em to the feed corral. Besides, I got a personal engagement with my nine friends at the Club Saloon."

"That's all right, Gimp. I won't detain you more'n a minute," said Dodge. "Can you make those ten friends of yours do anything you want 'em to do?"

"Well, I could by lickin' 'em, if I was able to lick 'em," Gimpy said doubtfully. "They're a bunch of fair-minded men, though. Tell you somethin' if you'll keep it plumb secret."

"I swear to God. Shoot," Lou Dodge ordered.

Whereupon Gimpy explained that he and his nine friend were going to stick up George Villard some time during the night to get money for to-morrow.

"That won't be robbin' him, will it, Lou?" Gimpy begged. "The old son-of-a-bitch owes us five dollars apiece anyway. We worked just as hard partin' his cattle away from the Double W cattle as we did partin' the Double W cattle away from his cattle. That won't be robbery, will it?"

"It most damned certainly won't," said Lou Dodge. "It'll merely be collecting what's rightfully due you. 'Course, I suppose you'd use a little pressure."

"I don't know what pressure is, Lou, but if the old son-of-a-bitch don't cough it up, we'll take it away from him. We all agreed on that. You'll keep this close under your hat, won't you?"

"It's an inviolable secret, Gimp," said Lou Dodge. "Don't you worry a minute about that. Now, here's my proposition. If you and your friends want to pick up a little extra money, I'll see to it personally that you get twenty-five dollars out of it."

"Dodge, that's a lot of money. What do you want, Lou?"

Dodge began explaining that Wallace had forbidden his daughter Enid to even so much as speak to Jim Villard.

"That there ain't right, Lou," Gimpy interrupted. "Jim Villard's just as good as that girl Enid is, and I know, 'cause I once rid for the Double W. Course she's pretty, but she's plumb spiled—most as spiled as a beef that's been dead for a month, and as for Jim Villard, he's white even if he is a goddamned Villard. Jim, he's a nice feller. Lou, I'd like to do somethin' fine for him because he treated me nice when I rid for the Circle 22 about a month. Dobie Dick Donovan, he fired me. What you want me to do?"

Though Lou Dodge was the local justice of the peace, he carefully explained that he wanted Gimpy and his nine companions to—in some manner—kidnap Bill Wallace and scare him into consenting for his daughter Enid to marry Jim Villard. He didn't care how the ten went about it as long as they accomplished it. Could they do it?

"Sure, sure, we can do it!" Gimpy agreed happily. "Hell, us ten can do anything. Do you want us to punish him proper if he won't agree at first? Now, this is what I call stickin' my horn into romance. I'll put this up to the other nine, Lou, and they'll agree all right, just as soon as I can get these horses to the feed corral. Hand some of the reins up to me as soon as I climb my saddle. By gosh, Lou, I never tackled a proposition in my life I couldn't do!"

"Well, that's why I picked you out for this delicate business, Gimp," Lou Dodge said confidentially. "The truth is, there isn't another man in Nevada I'd trust for a delicate job like this. Here, I'll help you get these horses to movin'."

A few minutes after Gimpy and his clumsy, almost unmanageable string of saddle-horses disappeared in the direction of the feed corral, Brazos Cobb and Dobie Dick Donovan breasted their horses up to the hitchrail in front of the Oriental Saloon about the middle of the main block. They swung down, their hairy chaparrejos making them clumsy.

As they stamped into the saloon, making plenty of noise with their spurs and their high-heeled boots, fourteen men already in the place left the bar and their chairs. One shouted in a frightened voice:

"Hell, boys, here are two mortal enemies. If they're goin' to do their shootin' in here, let's get out!"

In the space of about fourteen seconds the fourteen erstwhile patrons of the Oriental Saloon had all but broken the batwing doors from their hinges in getting themselves out of the place.

Big Norman, the bartender, brother of Gimpy, was pasty of face, his mouth open with fear because he knew of the mortal enmity of these two.

"Set aside a bottle and some glasses, Norm," Brazos ordered in a very friendly voice. "We're busy cow waddies for a couple of days and when our work's done, then we're goin' to do our shootin'. How does good, straight whisky suit you, Dobie?"

"Why, it suits me just fine, Brazos, my dear old friend," Dobie Dick said with real affection in his voice. "We'll lift a pair apiece and then we'll go to the Astor and wash up and eat a fine big supper in the dining-room. How about it, Norm, are these drinks on the house?"

"Yes, yes, of course, of course," Norm panted, realising with a great deal of relief that they were not going to shoot it out as soon as they got their drinks. "Anything you get in here to-night, boys, will be on the house. How about a few good cigars?"

"Yes, thanks," agreed Brazos Cobb; "give us a box of your best cigars, Norm."

"Yes, make it a box, Norm," added Dobie Dick Donovan, who had several notches on his gun handle. "With these couple of days of hard work, Brazos and me'll be too busy to roll our own, 'sides, I always did like to chew good cigars. They make plenty of spit."

CHAPTER EIGHT

THE CATTLE, which had been run for several miles during the cutting out operation, were left in a highly emotional state of mind, if beef steers ever became emotional. They were restless, undecided, and the wind blowing from the direction of the river and bringing with it the smell of water, added nothing to their steadiness.

The Sage Town youths, who imagined themselves seasoned cowboys, managed to hold the cattle, until a huge black bulk began to crawl through the blackness. It was nothing but a big load of loose hay drawn by a span of horses, but the cattle did not know that. The few more than a thousand steers began to move restlessly toward the river in a gathering stampede when the six riders raced around to that side and blocked their way. At the same time a vagrant changing of the wind brought to the nostrils of the steers the smell of dry, wild hay as the man on top of the first load began to fork hay off into the sagebrush.

Where a minute before the hungry, weary cattle had wanted only water and quiet, now they wanted only feed. In a bawling, but well-scattered band, they headed for the hay wagon, completely surrounding it and certainly stopping its progress until the second wagon showed up in the darkness.

Presently the drivers of the two outfits managed to again get their teams into motion, and this movement, coupled with the forking off of hay, strung the cattle out in a line perhaps a quarter of a mile long, or rather in two lines as the teamsters did not parallel each other.

" Now, boys," declared one of the would-be cowboys, who was only seventeen, " it's time for us to ride into town and wet our whistles and get something to eat. These here beef'll bed down as soon as they finish up that hay, and they won't move all night. What you say we hightail it? "

" But who'll sell us whisky in town? " demanded another would-be cowboy, who was only sixteen. " We can't get any whisky unless we get it from old Hankins, who makes his livin' sellin' it to the Injuns. My dad says that Injun likker's pisen."

They trotted away through the sagebrush and the darkness arguing about the virtue and purity of Injun whisky. By the time they crossed the rails, they had five to one decided to go home and get supper and some hot coffee, and to be back on night herd around ten or eleven o'clock, because the hungry steers could not fill their bellies before that time.

At about the time the six would-be cowboys decided to leave the herd to its own devices, Jim Villard, in his brushed off range clothes, with a new scarf about his deeply tanned neck, and with perfumed oil on his recently combed blond hair, unlatched the gate of the picket fence that surrounded blacksmith Edwards' front yard. The gravel walk was short so he made it with a few strides, lifted himself up the two steps of the porch and rapped upon the front door. There was quick noise inside and then the door opened, showing Lottie Edwards dimly silhouetted in the light of a kerosene lamp in the dining-room.

"Why, if it isn't Jim Villard!" Lottie gasped in simulated surprise, as she had been expecting just such a visit as this. "Won't you step in, or would you rather have her come out?"

She managed to refrain from asking whether Jim's father knew he was making this call.

"Enid," she said in a loud whisper. "There's a gentleman here to see you."

Enid Wallace, who had been standing about four feet to Lottie's left in the shadow, came out quickly, uttered a happy, yet nevertheless tearful cry, and wrapped her arms about Jim Villard's neck, and he lost less than no time in fervently embracing her. Their lips met, met again and again, continued to meet until Lottie, who was envious, jealous and quivering all over, managed to ask young Mr. Villard whether he'd had supper.

In the dining-room, where the Edwards family lived much of the time, the blacksmith and his wife looked quizzically at each other, silently asked whether they would get into trouble by having Jim Villard call upon Enid Wallace at their house.

"And what the hell if we do?" Edwards growled. "I'm beholden to neither of those men. If the lad cares to visit here, it's all right with me."

"Well, it's all right with me," his wife said snappishly. "I ain't agoin' to let a couple of old fools like Bill Wallace and George Villard tell me what I got to do in my own house. Tom, call to the young man to come on in. I hear 'em talkin' about that at the front door. I'll stir up the kitchen stove fire."

" Say you, Jim Villard," the blacksmith bawled. " Come on in and put on the nosebag. I heard you say you ain't et."

The three came in then, Jim with his arm about Enid's supple waist, and Lottie marching ahead looking a very lonesome lady who had no young man to escort her into her own house.

Enid's face was almost as red as the proverbial beet, and though she tried to disengage herself, she failed.

" Doggone it, Enid," Jim told her, " these folks all know we're goin' to get married as soon as we can. Likely they know I've hugged you many times before."

" Well, you needn't do it again here in public! " she blazed, but had to laugh.

" Well, howdy, Jim," greeted the blacksmith as he got a hold of Jim Villard's big, brown, right hand. " Glad to see you, but mighty sorry to hear there was some trouble over which outfit was to load first. Didn't go up to see how it was because from what I heard all the rest of the town was over there by the shippin' pens. Any truth in the report that Dobie Dick Donovan and that ornery little Texan named Brazos Cobb had a kind of a quarrel? "

" Oh, it was just a quarrel and didn't amount to anything," Jim said. " It was this way. Brazos, he knocks Dobie out of his saddle with his six-shooter, but when I saw them a few minutes ago, they had their boots on the bar rail in the Oriental and were toastin' the health of each other with a pair of whiskys. They're all right now, and Enid's father has his cattle on the way to San Francisco in spite of a couple of his cowboys."

Mrs. Edwards waddled in then, adding her greetings and her questions to those of her husband's.

" Yes, Mrs. Edwards," said Jim. " I reckon everything will go on all right from now on. I just come down for a minute or two to see whether Enid was all right."

" Yes, for a minute or two," Edwards said with forced

gravity. "Don't stay longer'n that, on account of what I hear the male parents of you two are threatenin' to do."

"Oh, darn my male parent!" flared Enid. "I'm old enough to know what I'm doin', and so is Jim. Mrs. Edwards, don't you go to a bit of trouble. I'll fix Jim something to eat if you'll let me use your kitchen."

"And I'll help, Mother," said Lottie, determined not to let these two do all their lovemaking without a witness present. "Come right on, Jim. We won't go to a bit of trouble for you. How do you like your beefsteak?"

"Oh, for God's sake, don't even say beefsteak to me," Jim said and grinned. "All I've heard for the last six months has been beef, beef, and more beef. Give me a can of sardines, and some crackers and cheese and a gallon of strong coffee."

"But we haven't any sardines, Jim," Lottie faltered, "but I can run to the Dodge store and get some. We have got plenty of canned oysters, though."

"Then oyster soup it is for me!" Jim approved, capturing Enid again with a long arm about her waist. "Oyster soup and crackers with plenty of black coffee. Got any cake, Lottie? If you ain't got cake, pie'll do. You say you got both pie and cake? Enid, be still. You let her cook and you sit on my knee."

"I will not!" the daughter of the owner of the Double W cried out, and broke free. "I guess I know how to cook."

"From the way that sounds to me," said Edwards, in the dining-room, "it looks like they know each other mighty well already."

"And you, bein' a man, would say somethin' like that, Edwards," his wife whispered angrily. "Ain't seen each other for four months to my knowledge, and Enid, I got to admit, is as slender as a willow wand. What puts such foul notions as that into your fool head, Edwards?"

"Him wantin' her to sit on his lap while Lottie cooked him some supper!"

" He didn't say that! He said knee. Has your memory reached such a point of degeneration, Edwards, that you've forgot that I sat on your lap more than once before we were married? "

" Well, now you remind me of it, maybe you did. Want to set over here now, sweetheart? This here love makin' by the young is always mighty contagious to me."

" No, I don't and you're an old fool! Don't forget we've got a growed-up daughter."

In the Edwards' kitchen, while the three young people talked and laughed and cooked and then ate, all of them partaking of oyster stew, they managed to formulate a plan, which they would put into execution if their happiness was interrupted by the appearance of Bill Wallace or Villainous George Villard. They were still whispering and talking and eating cake and pie when Edwards said he had to work hard and was going to bed. Would his wife come with him?

" Well, I guess I will, Tom," she said with forced reluctance. " They'll talk till midnight. I'll look in on 'em and see whether they're going to leave us anything for breakfast, and if they are I'll join you soon."

Gimpy, having managed to deliver the ten saddled horses at the feed corral and telling the hostler to take care of them, found his nine confederates with as many boots on the iron footrail of the Oriental Saloon. Bursting with importance now, Gimpy grinned a sickly grin and tried to be sober, reserved and conservative.

" Here's the damned idiot now," shouted Johnny Granger. " Fill him up a glass. Handle those ten broncs all right, Gimp? "

" Sure, I did, Johnny," Gimpy declared and snickered as, with a shaking hand, he took the filled glass and quickly emptied it. " Didn't have a bit of trouble. I could lead a hundred horses if I had to do it. No, I don't want another drink now. Always make it a habit never to drink much on an empty belly, but let me get my belly full and I'll drink you all under the table."

"Like hell you will," disagreed Tommy Jones. "That's what these fellows have been tryin' to do with me."

Nine slightly inebriated cowboys demanded to be told in detail what Gimpy had been doing and why he had been gone so long. Gimpy declared mysteriously that he'd explain nothing in such a public place as the Oriental Saloon. He would die before he'd explain a word. He would tell all about it, however, after they'd filled their bellies with the Chinaman's grub.

"Oh, let's go along with him," warbled Windy Wallace, who was a distant relative of Bill Wallace, owner of the Double W range and about five thousand cattle. "The damned idiot's got his neck bowed.

"And I'm for shootin' him," said Johnny Granger, "but I'll tag along. Are we goin' to have another round before we leave?"

"I think," Tommy Jones said judiciously, "that we've had plenty for the present. We got to have cool heads to hear about that bargain Gimpy seems to have made for us."

Gimpy led off, pushing grandly past the bat-wing doors, but he was surrounded by his nine friends and confederates as soon as they gained the irregular boardwalk. Gimpy refused to tell them anything, however, until they were in the middle of the dusty side street beyond the corner of Morton's big general store, and about fifty yards from the lit up, if lonely looking, Chinaman's restaurant.

"Puke it up, Gimp, or I'll cut it out of you!" ordered Johnny Granger. "Spill the beans!"

"Or we'll choke it out of the crazy bastard," added Hap Lawson. "Stop swellin' your flabby chest so big, Gimp. Let out your breath in words we can understand."

"Now, she's this way, boys," Gimpy began with all the importance he could command. "It's a really big bargain I've made with Lou Dodge. He showed me a mighty lot of respect by lettin' me make the bargain for all you other fellers."

"Well, I don't want anybody to make my bargains," said Windy Wallace and his eight fellow cowboys agreed.

"But there's money in this here bargain I made for you fellows and myself," Gimpy argued. "Big money! There's twenty-five dollars."

Voice tight with suppressed excitement, Gimpy told them that Lou Dodge would pay them twenty-five dollars hard cash if they would scare old Villainous Villard into consenting to allow his son Jim to marry Enid Wallace.

"And that there ain't all, friends," Gimpy added by way of embellishment. "We got to scare the mean old son-of-a-bitch until he agrees to give 'em a grand weddin', with a preacher and bridesmaids and wine and the like and plenty beans. Lou insists on it."

"Then Lou Dodge is sure my friend," yipped Hap Lawson.

"And me," declared Johnny Granger. "I'm through punchin' cattle! From now on I'm goin' to be a diplomat and a schemer. This is makin' money a lot easier than punchin' cows. Ain't that your New Year's resolution, Tom?"

"But, dammit, this here ain't New Year!" Gimpy stammered. "It's only early October. You fellers are all drunk. Are you sure you got the details of that bargain Lou Dodge has made with me?"

"Gimp, listen to me," Tommy Jones ordered with much gravity. "Don't you think you got things bassackwards? Are you sure it's old Villard we got to scare? Jim Villard, he's a man. He's got a right to do as he likes if he bows his neck. Don't Lou Dodge want us to scare Bill Wallace so he'll consent for his girl to marry a Villard? Ain't that the way Lou told it to you?"

"By God, it is, boys!" Gimpy stammered, then snickered. "That's the trouble with me. I've got the off horse on the near side. That's right, boys, Lou says he'll pay us twenty-five dollars hard cash if we'll scare old

Bill Wallace into agreein' for his girl Enid to marry Jim Villard. That's the bargain which I made for you fellers, it bein' all right with me from the start. How are we goin' to do it?"

Then there followed much talk in which strangely Tom Jones did not join. He voiced his thoughts only when he discovered there were nine different opinions on how to scare Bill Wallace to death.

"Silence, you damned noise bags!" Tom ordered grandly. "Harken unto me and listen. You men go on to the Chinaman's and order grub. I'm goin' into Morton's store there and buy ten new bed-sheets."

"Ten new bed-sheets!" Gimpy stuttered. "Say, Tom, how many women are you goin' to bed with? What the hell do you want with more'n one bed-sheet?"

"My dear Gimpy," said Tom Jones, reproachfully but very gravely, "I'm goin' to get ten bed-sheets so we can have ten napkins when we eat grub yonder at the Chinaman's."

"Well, doggone it," Gimpy stammered, then snickered. "I done forgot we'd need napkins at the Chinaman's—me not bein' much used to napkins. I generally lick my fingers, or rub the gravy off on my pants. You go right along."

"After you nine dig up about a dollar apiece," Jones objected. "I'll chip in my own dollar. If there's anything I do like when I go into an eatin' house it's a big napkin, sheet size. Dig me up nine dollars. If I can buy 'em cheaper, you'll get back your change. Order me ham and eggs and hotcakes and half a dried apple pie."

After the lighting of numerous matches to facilitate the making of change, Tom got the nine dollars, which he dropped tingingly into a pocket, then he announced that he had to have ninety cents more as he had to buy ten new bandannas—of course, he would pay for his own. Johnny Granger said that he had a dirty one around his neck and a snotty one in his back pocket.

" Yes, you do," disagreed Tom. " You hombres seem to have forgot that Villainous Villard owes us fifty dollars."

" By gosh, that's right, ain't it? " the gathering agreed. " Somebody light a match 'till we find ninety cents. Oh, hell, light two matches."

Sullen, sour of heart as a cucumber pickled in straight vinegar, filled with self-pity, filled with hate for everybody by the name of Wallace, George Villard sat and shivered in his upstairs bedroom of the Astor House until he was certain he could get supper alone in the dining-room, because in spite of all of the travail and worry of the day, he was ravenously hungry.

Descending to the ground floor by the back stairs, he entered the kitchen, where an old and wrinkled China-man presided over a very large and hot range in a very smelly atmosphere. Villard stamped on regardless of the salutation of the Chinaman, who demanded that he tell him what he wanted to eat. Seeing that the dining-room was entirely empty, Villard felt as though he'd been happily warmed by a single ray of sunshine. Gertie Watson, a middle-aged and homely waitress, came, a little in awe, and asked him what he'd have for supper. Glowering at her Villard gave his order, and she waddled away, telling herself that he was a mighty mean man, and that he did not deserve having such a nice young man as Jim Villard for his son.

" Damned old mean polecat! " Gertie said by way of emphasis. " If he was my father I'd shoot him some dark night and let the coyotes eat him."

The rich owner of the Circle 22 had eaten about half of his fried beefsteak and about half of his greasy fried potatoes, when in jingled Brazos Cobb and Dobie Dick Donovan, arm in arm because they were a trifle unsteady on their feet. Villard's first reaction was one of incredu-lity, but the next moment he was scrambling irately to his feet as this spectacle of his gun-slinging wagon boss and that damned killer of a wagon boss from the Double W acting as fraternal as if they were blood brothers.

" Don't let us bother you, Villainous," advised Brazos. " There's plenty of room for us at your table and our bellies are empty."

" Sure, and don't let us run you off, Mr. Villard," advised Dobie Dick. " This here little runty son-of-a-bitch and me, we're on perfectly friendly terms now. We guarantee we won't start a fight. Will we, Brazos? "

" Nah, we won't start trouble, Villainous," Brazos reassured with a sneer. " There's too damned much work ahead of us to start trouble to-night."

Out went Villard, but not until he'd grabbed his hat.

" And now, by drat," he inanely soliloquised as he gained the boardwalk. " I'll go down to that Chinese restaurant and enjoy my supper in peace and tranquility, which I rightfully deserve. By drat, I'll fire Dobie Dick Donovan for associatin' with that dratted, gun-throwin', wagon boss of the Double W! By drat, I'll do that if it's the last act of my life, even if he does know more about cattle than any other man in Nevada! "

CHAPTER NINE

SIGHING LIKE weary, full-bellied men, the ten cowboys straggled from the Chinese Restaurant. Some had cigarettes already going. Others were rolling them as they travelled. In the lead was Tommy Jones, carrying a tightly wrapped paper bundle. It contained the ten new bed-sheets, which, he had explained while they were eating, were to be used later. As for the ten bandannas they had been given to as many cowboys, and each, following Jones's instructions, had tied one about his neck in such a manner that it could be pulled up to the eyes, if, as Tom explained: " The dust gets to flyin' so thick you can't breath nothin' but dust."

Tom was sucking-in the inhalation of cigarette smoke, when suddenly he stiffened. Out went his cigarette, the fire end rubbed vigorously in palm of tough left hand.

" Douse those glims, boys," he ordered. " Put 'em out! Don't show a light! "

" I'm goin' to light my smoke," Gimpy declared. " I'm a free man."

" You douce that glim, or you're a dead man, Gimp! " Tommy Jones said. " That goes for the rest of you, too. Here, take this."

From man to man, like the working of a bucket brigade at the village fire, the bundle of sheets was passed back until Hap Lawson, who was just coming out of the door, threw it at the Chinaman."

" Take care of that, you Chink! We'll get 'em later."

" All light," said the imperturbable Chinaman, catching the bundle.

Jones moved quickly out of the light that shone out of the Chinaman's one window. His confederates followed him into the shadows, demanding to be told whether he'd suddenly gone loco. Jones made a quick gesture toward the opposite side of the side street and whispered:

" There's the old varmint right over there, like he was walkin' into a trap. Pull up your bandannas! "

Across the side street, standing almost in front of Morton's big general store, was none other than George Villard, what was left of the lone light that had been left in the store outlining him just enough to make his identity certain.

" Let's surround the old bastard! " Johnny Granger whispered. " Say, do you think he's suspectin' anything?"

" If he does," Jones reassured, " it's the wrong thing. Maybe he's lookin' for a missin' son."

" He's a son-of-a-bitch if he's a Villard," Gimpy corrected and snickered. " Say, where do you reckon Jim Villard is? "

" Oh, he's wherever Enid Wallace is," Windy Wallace

said sarcastically. "You can bet your last white chip on that, Gimp."

"Well, of all the luck," Hap Lawson chuckled. "If he ain't a cross between a de-horned old bull and an ornery she-jackass. Shall we spread out and surround him, Tommy?"

"Just wait a minute, now," Jones ordered, with the authority of a general. "We'll wait and see what his next move is to be. The old devil's comin' right across the street. I know why. He's figured out he can get a cheaper supper with the Chinaman than he can at either hotel."

The cold autumn sky blazed with stars, some of which seemed as large as the heads of whisky barrels. There would have been complete silence but for the slow exhaust of the steam pump lifting water into the railroad tank, and the occasional bawl of a steer well beyond the shipping pens. Villard, as if making a sudden decision, started to step from the walk when to his right, perhaps forty feet away, two dogs sprang into vicious and noisy combat.

"Look at the old varmint jump!" yipped Gimpy. "Likely he figured a grizzly bear had bit him on the butt."

"Shut up, you idiot!" Tommy Jones ordered.

Then as if a dog fight were beneath the notice of such a rich and powerful man as he, Villard began to dogtrot across the dark street.

As he did this, a dark group of men loomed out of the shadows at one side of the Chinaman's restaurant and began to advance quickly. The ten cowboys were upon the owner of the Circle 22 before he could stop and decide what to do. They spread into units of five, surrounded him and closed in. Something small and hard jabbed him in the belly so hard it made him utter a grunt. Then from behind his bandanna mask, Tom Jones spoke sharply and gruffly, saying this:

"Mister, we don't give a damn who you are or what you are, it's money or your life! Pay up or die!"

"By drat, I deliver my money to no man, or group of men!" Villard stormed, trying to free his arms in order that he could wave them. "Stand aside and let me pass. In case you don't know who I am, I'm George Villard, owner of the great Circle 22 ranch. As I've told you, I deliver my money to no man unless I owe it to him, and by drat, I refuse to pay him unless he asks me for it like a gentleman."

"Oh, hell, we don't care if you own a hundred Circle 22 ranches, mister," Jones growled from deep in his chest. "What we want is our money—enough to allow us to grab the next freight train comin' through that'll take us to Salt Lake City."

"The old liar," Gimpy suddenly shrilled. "Hell, he owes us fifty and he knows it! Let's search his pockets!"

"Shut up, you damned idiot!" Hap Lawson yipped, poking Gimpy in his flat belly with a sharp elbow. "What do you want to do, put us all in jail for about ten years?"

"Choke that damned fool to death back there!" Jones growled, keeping the muzzle of his six-shooter pressed against Villard's middle. "He's just a piece of flotsam——belongs here in this town. He picked on us because he thinks he can get to be a professional hobo like we are."

"Hell, he don't know what he's talking about," Gimpy whispered tightly. "He's still drunk."

"And you'll be dead, Gimp!" Hap hissed at him, jabbing at him again with his elbow. "Keep your damned mouth shut! Chew on that new bandanna."

Pushing Gimpy to the outside of the ring, the nine riders closed in, each in a deep and guttural voice telling what he was going to do to this man if this man didn't dig up fifty dollars and in a hurry.

Threatening, wishing that he had the courage to take the name of the Deity in vain, Villard declared that he paid no debt unless it were an honest debt. He'd die before he'd be robbed! Let these villainous men take themselves from him.

"And him talkin' about us bein' villainous," snickered Gimpy. "And that bein' his nickname, and he deserves it."

"Shut up, you idiot!" growled Johnny Granger. "Shut up, or I'll break your neck."

Guessing that they could accomplish nothing with Villard where they had him, Tom Jones ordered him gagged and blindfolded. This was quickly done, and not gently, with two dirty bandannas.

"Now, pick him up, four of you men," Jones growled. "We'll take him outside of town there apiece and build a fire under him."

"You may burn me, but not my soul!" Villard fumed through his gag. "I'll deliver my money to no gang of thugs."

"That's just what we are, mister," growled Jones. "We hopped off an eastbound freight awhile ago, figuring that this was a good town to make a stake in, and you look to us like our meat. Goin' to settle for fifty dollars?"

"By drat, not for fifty cents!" Villard cried, trying to shout through his gag. "Not even for a dime."

He struggled fiercely to get free, but in vain, because he was being carried by four cowboys, who had a hold of his legs and arms and shoulders. Tom Jones gaily led the procession, which he directed toward the bridge that spanned the river about a mile away. Johnny Granger was the first to begin wearying of walking with high-heeled boots on. He suggested they put their victim down just outside the edge of town and there build a fire under him.

"No, none of that," Jones vetoed in that deep, guttural voice. "We'll take him to the river and drown him, after we've took everything in his pockets."

"But the river," Johnny complained and almost bit his tongue off to keep from mentioning the name of Tom Jones, "the river, it's an awful long way to walk."

"Then get down and crawl," Jones growled. "We've

got a fat prize here, chum, and we can't afford to let him go. At the bridge, we'll rifle his pockets and then tie him hand and foot and throw him over. That's what we'll do with this pilgrim."

They had the still angry, but much more frightened, owner of the Circle 22 about two hundred yards clear of the northerly side of the village on the road to the river, when he managed to make himself intelligible through his gag, and to temporise and bargain. If they would free him he would pay them ten dollars, but not a dratted cent more!

" Gather up some rocks, chums," Tom Jones growled. " If you can't find rocks, pick up pieces of scrap iron or anything. We want to weight his pockets down when we take his money out. He's so damned stingy we'll have to drown him. I've shot men and knifed men, but never before have I drowned men, but it's got to be done to him."

" Then let's get goin' and do it," growled Windy Wallace. " We've got to catch the next westbound freight out of here. Tell you what, chums, I won't feel safe 'till I've grabbed the guts of a high dangler."

" What's one of them things? " whispered Gimpy, who was bringing up the tailend of the procession. " Never heard of one of them high danglers before."

" Oh, it's just a damned freight boxcar," jeered Hap Lawson, who was next in procession. " That's hobo talk, Gimp. By guts he means the rods under the freight car."

" What's the matter up front? Is that hobo that's leadin' us gettin' weak in the knees? "

" This here knight of the road is gettin' strong in the knees," growled Jones. " This old varmint is offerin' to settle with us for an even fifty if we spare his life."

" Take his fifty but drown him anyway," said Hap Lawson, growling like an enraged grizzly. " Drown him if he won't make it a hundred."

" But damn it, he don't owe us a hundred," Gimpy snickered. " He don't owe us but fifty."

" Shut up, you damned fool, do you want to give the whole show away? Let Tom do the bargainin'."

" And you, Hap," Gimpy stammered roughly, " you done called him Tom.

In that moment George Villard was too busy in bargaining and trying to free himself to overhear.

" All right, all right," Tom growled. " We'll settle for an even fifty, you old geezer. That'll be enough to see us through to 'Frisco. Let me tell you this, though. If you strike a light to give us the right change, we'll cut your throat and take all the money you've got and then take you to the river and drown you."

They set Villard on his feet then and moved away from him a little to give him room to get at his purse. The men, peering over the upper edges of their bandanna masks, could faintly see him fumbling first in one pocket, then in another.

" Maybe the old son-of-a-bitch carries a gun," Gimpy whispered fearfully.

" No, I patted him," Jones reassured. " He's the kind that's too damned stingy to tote a gun for fear it'd cost him somethin'. I'll inform him again if he don't pay up mighty soon, he'll be short one life. I'm holdin' my hand out, rich cattle man."

" Rich cattle man, hell," Gimpy sniffed. " Here's how I size him up. He only owns one steer and one cow. Seems to me I saw him shovellin' manure down at the edge of that feed corral. He's the same man, ain't he, chum? "

" He's the same man, chum," Tom growled as he felt a twenty-dollar piece put into his hand. " But you can never tell about these manure pitchers. The majority of them are awful misers. There's some of them that would eat hay and rob the horses of grain just to keep from spendin' ten cents. Thank you, miser, for the fifty."

Giving a prearranged signal, Tom poked the fifty into an overall's pocket. Tom saw his nine companions disappear in nine directions and gave the victim this advice:

"Miser man, if you pull off that blindfold in less than ten minutes, you'll be shot clean through the heart, and, by God, I'll do it. I'll be lingerin' right off there by the edge of the road to see you don't unblindfold yourself. Thank you for the fifty."

Then stamping off the gravel road, and certainly making plenty of noise, Tom stopped, staring at the form of the man standing stiff in the middle of the road. Then cowboy Tom Jones strode softly away, taking the tenth direction.

"Stingy, hard-bitten old varmint!" Tom chuckled when he was well out of hearing. "He gave up that fifty like an ordinary man would give up both eyes."

Then Tom discovered that he and his confederates had a distressing problem on their hands. Possibly they should give this fifty to Bill Wallace, but how in the hell were they going to do it without confessing that they had taken the fifty away from George Villard.

"Oh, I reckon we'll keep it," Tom said happily, when he quickly reached a decision. "It won't be much trouble for each of us to spend five dollars more."

As George Villard stood there in the road, shivering a little from the relief and the cold, he tried to count off the seconds by the tumultuous thumping of his heart. Never before had he spent such a long ten minutes. Still, being blindfolded gave him an opportunity to surmise and conjecture the promise of slow and certain death by the men who had robbed him. On one point he was certain. They had worn spurs. The next moment, however, he was deciding that this knowledge did him no good, because the disreputable thieving hobos might have worn spurs as part of a disguise.

George Villard had most certainly not given up the fifty dollars with any semblance of pleasure. That was his deepest wound, and one about half as deep had been caused by his having been called a manure pitcher in a feed corral.

"Drat it, drat it," he cursed, wanting terribly much to

do some real swearing. " I could buy all the feed corrals in the west and have money left. Me, George Villard, accused of pitchin' manure in a feed corral! "

There came to him then the recollection of his having done such dirty and menial work in laying the corner-stone for his fortune. He tried to shrug that memory away. He wanted to forget it forever, but one thing he was not going to forget—that was vengeance. He'd find Sheriff Andy Smith and set Andy on the trail of these bandits before a freight train went through to take them out of the sheriff's jurisdiction.

Walking very fast, he changed his mind by the time he reached the railroad station, because he was remembering that once Andy Smith had told him to his face that he wouldn't believe a damned thing he said.

" Better forget the whole thing," he muttered right-eously under his breath. " I'll make up the loss by cuttin' my men by five dollars a month each until I get the fifty back."

He was lighter of heart, a little more in peace of mind as he set out by a circuitous route to reach the back stairs of the Astor House in order that he could gain his room unseen.

He was in the black alley back of the hotel when he was stopped in his tracks by a horrifying, soul-shattering thought, such a thought as to leave his self-righteousness grown to ten times its normal size. Had his son, his own son, his only son, been one of those thieving thugs? That might be true, because that son made a practice of wearing his long-shanked spurs while in town.

" Oh, God grant he was not, God grant he was not," Villard silently prayed as he felt his way toward the bottom of the rear stairs. " I'll make the young scamp into confessing about it to me, though."

Just about the time Villard gained the safety and comparative warmth of his sparsely furnished bedroom, again the cowboys were together at a prearranged rendezvous in the sagebrush about a hundred yards east of the feed corral and livery stable. They were unmasked now, and each of them had vigorously rubbed his new bandanna in the dirt so it would no longer look new.

"Gimp, you go get the bundle from the Chinaman," Tom ordered in natural voice. "While you're gone the rest of us will stay here and palaver. I got a pint flask."

"Then I ain't agoin' a damn' step till I get a drink out of it," Gimp said. "You fellows have abused me awful and I want a drink to make me feel better."

"Here, take a little one, Gimpy. I'll hold the flask. You ain't got sense enough to know what a moderate drink is, and this pint's got to go all the way around."

Gimpy came trotting in out of the darkness, his run-over high-heeled boots making scuffing marks in the dry dirt. As he made out his confederates in the black blur, he came to an abrupt stop.

"Durn it, men," he growled. "I had a damned good notion to eat another supper so I could use one of these sheets for a napkin. We plumb forgot to do that, didn't we?"

"Oh, you damned idiot," Jones growled. "We didn't intend to use them sheets for napkins. Each of us is goin' to take one of them and make a ghost out of himself."

"Ghost! I ain't agoin' to make no ghost out of myself!" Gimpy disagreed. "I been a robber to-night and I'm proud of it, and I'm damned if I'm goin' to be a ghost!"

As though Gimpy was a hundred miles away, Jones began to explain how they'd all have to patrol the town so somebody'd be on hand to apprehend Bill Wallace when he sneaked out of his hole.

"Which hole?" demanded Gimpy. "Which hole did that old son-of-a-bitch crawl into anyway?"

"Oh, you idiot," drawled Hap Lawson. "We're talkin' about his room in the Empire Hotel. We got a hunch that sometimes before mornin' he'll sneak out."

"Say, did any of you fellers happen to see what becomes of Villard? Seems to me as I cut across here I seen somebody hightailin' it into that alley back of the hotel. I don't think it matters much, as he'll be scared we'll kill him if he says anything about it."

"Now tell me, boys," said Gimpy as he hitched along on his haunches to get in the middle of the other nine squatting men. "Tell this to me so a wise man can understand it. Is it our plan for each of us to wear a sheet so we can scare Bill Wallace once he comes out of his hole?"

"Yes, that's the big idea, Gimp," reassured Johnny Granger. "And if the old son-of-a-bitch don't come out of his hole, we're going in and pull him out. Don't you want to go along with us on those terms?"

"By gosh, I sure do!" Gimpy declared and snickered loudly. "Give me a sheet and I'll be a ghost—as for napkins, I never did like the damned things! Where's my sheet? I want to put it on and see how I look as a ghost."

"Now don't rattle your hocks so they make too much noise, Gimp," Tom Jones ordered. "Each man's to carry his sheet inside his shirt until we definite locate Bill Wallace. I'll be superintendin' the whole business. Here's your sheet, Gimp. Pull out your shirt tail and wrap it around your body and poke in your shirt tail again. The rest of you hombres do the same thing."

CHAPTER TEN

IN THE WARM Edwards' kitchen, Jim Villard and Enid Wallace began to suspect that they could talk much more pleasantly if alone, though they both liked Lottie. They naturally couldn't order her out of her own house.

Neither wanted to go uptown because there would be much drinking in the saloons and doubtless cowboys travelling from saloon to saloon. Then there was the matter of their respective fathers. They certainly did not want to meet them.

" Damn it," Jim said under his breath, " why doesn't Lottie go to bed? If I knew where I could find her a young man who wasn't drunk, I'd sure bring him."

Soon after that Enid said, with a stretch and a convincing yawn, that because she had eaten so much and the warmth of the kitchen she was having a hard time keeping her eyes open. Jim knew he should have a convincing answer to that, but at the moment he could not find it.

" Jim, I can't stand this any longer, and keep awake," Enid said. " If you and Lottie will excuse me, I'll go out in the cold and walk around a little."

She told him with her eyes that she did not want to go alone.

" Go ahead, both of you," Lottie said. " If I had a sweetheart here, I'd want to be alone with him. Take along a wrap, it's chilly outside. Here's my old wool coat. Jim, you're too range toughened to get cold in such weather as this."

Jim said that he did not need a wrap. He added that just being close to Enid kept him warm.

" Then I won't go outside with you, smart cowboy! " she flared. " If you think I'm that sort of a girl. I just won't."

" Bet you a dollar against a doughnut you go," Lottie offered. " I know I would if I were in your place."

" Well, you're not in my place, Lottie," Enid said and laughed. " Wait for me in the front room, Jim. I'll get Lottie's old coat."

Outside, under the cold stars, they walked slowly to and fro. They had much to say, but said little, seeming quite content to keep as close together as possible, Jim with an arm about her waist, she trying to see how far she could reach around his. Now and then, when they could give their attention to it, they heard faintly the noise from the main part of town.

" Jim, do you think there's any danger of Father coming looking for you? " she queried. " I wouldn't like anything to happen to embarrass the Edwards folks. They're so good to me."

"I don't believe the old cuss will look for me much to-night," Jim reassured. "I think he's too mad at my father."

"But don't you believe this cattle shipping business will end it?" she demanded, fear grabbing at her heart.

"Not with my father, I'm sorry to say, Enid," Jim amended quick. "After bein' licked once, how do you think your father will look at it?"

"He won't quit either," she said, uttering a little laugh that had more fear than mirth in it. "He'll just wait, likely, for your father to make the next move. Jim, my shoe's untied. Would you mind tying it? I'm so swaddled up in this big coat."

"Don't unswaddle," Jim reassured and dropped to one knee. "Of course, you've got on high shoes so I'll have to tie high."

"You tie low, Jim Villard!" she ordered considerably against her will. "I've just got on my pair of dancing pumps I keep at Lottie's house. That's my ankle, Mr. Villard. It's not untied."

She giggled and told herself she'd like to kick him as he fumbled for the ends of her shoestrings. He managed to retie the shoe without suffering serious bodily injury though he had to exert a great deal of will power.

"Enid, you sure got a shapely leg," he said soberly, after he'd regained his feet and kissed her. "I don't know that I ever felt a more shapely calf except a nice little red heifer I had to brand once."

"Thank you, Mr. Villard," she snapped, though she did blush so furiously she felt her face burn.

Lunging away from him, she opened the gate and marched in along the gravel path until he overtook her at the steps, swung her about and set her down upon the edge of the porch.

"Mad, honey?"

" No, not very mad," she confessed and laughed softly.

He sat down beside her, drew her tightly towards him and the next moment she fought away.

" Now, what's wrong? " he demanded, puzzled. " I just tickled you under the ear."

" And your darn moustache tickled me. Jim, why don't you shave off that thing? I don't like moustaches."

" Well, I suppose you're quite an authority on the tickling qualities of moustaches, Miss Wallace? "

" Sure I am, just as you seem to be quite a judge of shapely legs. Let's talk serious, and not get to quarrelling, Jim. Jim, would you marry me? "

" You're damned right I would! Haven't I told you that about a hundred and fifty times? "

" But I mean now! "

He jerked away from her, stared.

" Right now, this very minute? "

" You fool, of course not. It would take us an hour or two to get a licence and a judge. Jim, I'm willin' to be married by the justice of the peace—that is unless you want a preacher."

Being at an age when practically all humanity seemed more stubborn than sensible, she said that in her opinion the only way to settle the trouble between their fathers was for her and Jim to get married. What did he think about that?

" I ain't worryin' about what they do—that is to any big extent," he drawled as he drew her closely again. " Seems to me if we get married I won't have any troubles."

" Nor I! " she said quickly and emphatically. " Jim, I'll live just for you."

" And five or six brats," he corrected.

" Yes, for our children," she murmured. " Isn't it strange that we're thinking of children? "

" I don't know, seems to me most married people we know have kids. Let's forget about the brats, though, and get down to business talking about getting married. You can sure bet your last white chip on one thing. If you marry me, all the hell my stingy father can raise won't make any difference. Honey, tell me honestly, if it comes to a showdown will you side with your father?"

"Indeed I would not!" she flared out. "Jim, my father hasn't a thing against you except that you're George Villard's son. Do you happen to know how your father feels towards me—that is, deep down in his heart? He told me plenty plain to-day what he thought of me."

"You couldn't get very deep down in his heart, Enid," he said and wished he had not to say it. "His heart's about the size of a peanut and it's all one hard shell. Does your father feel the same way toward me?"

"Well, it's a cinch he don't love you. Do you see any reason in our fathers acting like such bull-headed old fools when we're so happy? Honey, let's get down to business and talk about when we are to get married."

Despite the peacefulness of the Edwards' home, Miss Lottie had a presentment that before many hours it would undergo an upheaval, and not a mild one. As a consequence of this presentiment, she did not turn in, which she wanted to do.

Slipping into the front room she turned up the wick of the kerosene lamp, sat down in her mother's rocking-chair and picked a magazine from the centre table.

Though she told herself she was going to read, she knew that was a lie. Presently she had a more comforting thought. She would be handy in case Enid's father came on a still hunt expecting his prey to be one, Jim Villard, or in case Villainous Villard came searching for his son, his purpose being to kick him all the way out of Nevada for being found in the company of that worthless Wallace girl.

"Gosh, I do hope something happens!" Lottie said to herself. "I'd sure like to get even with Villainous Villard for the names he called me because I scared that

steer with my red dress. If he comes here I'll give him
a piece of my mind, even if Jim is here, but it'd be a
heap better if he doesn't find Jim here. I'd like a chance
to tell Bill Wallace what I think of him, too, because he's
forbidden Enid to ever again speak to Jim Villard. What
fools those two old men are. Put together they haven't
sense enough to pound sand into a rat hole."

Sitting on the edge of the bed up in his cold room at the
Aster House, George Villard, with what he thought a
clarity of mind, tried to take stock of his situation. He
reluctantly admitted that he had suffered defeat at the
hands of Bill Wallace. That was an account that could
be balanced, and by tarnation, drat, he would balance
that before he quit the game!

He had been robbed! Ignominiously robbed by a band
of hobo thugs, anyone of which could have overpowered
him had he had the necessary courage.

" The damned cowardly reprobates! " Villard snarled.
" Saying it in plain words, they ganged up on me. If I
was doing my duty as a citizen, I'd report that outrage
to Sheriff Smith."

He just remembered that once Sheriff Smith, in the
presence of about a dozen other men, had told him he
was a damned cattle thief and should be in jail. That was
an insult that could never be forgiven, and most certainly
he was not going to give Andy Smith the opportunity to
capture ten hobo bandits. No, by tarnation, he wasn't!
If Smith was one-tenth a sheriff he would have seen to it
that such outlaws didn't even get off a freight train in
Big Sage.

He started to thinking of his son, Jim, as the one
rightful man to apprehend and punish those ten hobo
bandits. He did not think this way for long, however,
because his memory was good, and it was not difficult
for him to recollect that his son Jim had told him two
weeks ago that he would pay court to that damned worthless Enid Wallace any time he liked to do it.

He then began wondering where his son Jim was, and decided he was probably in one of the saloons drinking, talking, laughing, gambling.

In his hate and frustration, Villard's reasoning reached almost a frenzy in which he considered getting a knife or a gun, or both, and setting out to find Bill Wallace, and settling their differences man to man, frontier style.

Then there appeared a bright, burnished little spot in his memory which reminded him that he who lived by the sword, perished by the sword.

He had not been in bed much more than a minute before he told himself that it was much more sensible to let to-morrow take care of itself. This was retreating from his thoughts when he growled:

"By drat, tarnation, if I'd let the to-morrows of the past take care of themselves, where would I be now? Would I be the owner of five thousand cattle, and one of the best ranges in northern Nevada? By drat, no! Now, I'll go to sleep and take care of to-morrow when it comes."

He actually did. He was breathing heavily within five minutes, snoring within ten.

This was about the time that Bill Wallace decided that sleep was not for him that night. For an hour and a half he'd squirmed and turned over and over. No, sir, sleep would not be for him this night unless he paid a visit to his daughter at the Edwards' home, and while there if he happened to find Jim Villard, he would kick him all the way across the Humboldt River. No, by God, he'd kick him into the river and drown him. Hadn't he warned him enough not to pay attention to Enid?

"Well, if the young son-of-a-bitch is there," he soliloquised after he was fully dressed, "maybe I better take a gun along and shoot him and finish this distressin' business. Damned if I know why that daughter of mine is so infatuated with that young varmint, who anybody can see is just a young edition of Villainous Villard."

Convinced that he could go to sleep easily after he'd had a fatherly talk with Enid, Wallace decided against taking along a gun. If he found Jim Villard at the Edwards' home he might become so enraged that he'd shoot somebody by accident—possibly his own daughter, and fail to kill young Villard. With this thought in his mind, and no small determination, he set out, stopping only at the Club Saloon long enough to get a stiff drink of whisky to warm his physical body, not his courage.

It so happened that one of the dozen or more men standing at the bar was Pete Cummings, one of the ten who had robbed Villard.

"Oh, oh," he said to his empty whisky glass. "I'll trail him when he leaves. He's so damned mad about somethin' he doesn't even see me."

When Wallace stamped out, he had no thought of being followed, though Pete Cummings did amble along about thirty feet behind him.

At the corner, Wallace stepped from the tie walk, turned sharply and set off in the direction of the dark part of the village where the home of blacksmith Edwards was located.

Pete let him go about fifty yards in that direction, then placed two fingers to his lips and blew hard, uttering a soul-penetrating whistle. About thirty seconds later a man ran out of the alley that bisected that block.

"Where's the old son-of-a-bitch? Which way did he go?" Hap Lawson demanded gleefully. "That you, Pete? Did you see him, or are you drunk?"

"Put your ear to the ground, Hap, and you can hear him walkin'," Pete ordered. "Unless he changes his course, he'll wind up at the Edwards' house."

"But, gosh, that's where Enid's stayin'!"

"Which is a plumb good reason he's headin' for the Edwards' home," declared Pete.

"Say," whispered Hap. "That's where Jim Villard is. I sneaked up to the picket fence just about half an hour ago, and him and that Enid girl was settin' on the edge of the front porch, and hell, wasn't they makin' awful love! Just listenin' to that made me so much in love I had a mind to step in there and kill Jim Villard. Say, Pete, do you think it matters much which man makes love to a girl, as long as he's a man? I'd a done just as good as Jim Villard makin' love to Enid, wouldn't I? Give me your honest opinion on that controversial subject, Pete."

" Well, I'll give you an opinion on this," Pete said soberly. " We'd best summon the clan. Hap, you make sure old Wallace is headed for the Edwards' place, and I'll do some whistlin' to round up the rest of the boys."

" Jim, there's a man coming from towards town," Enid whispered tensely as she stiffened out of Jim's embrace, " and I think it's my father. I can recognise his walk just by hearing it. He'll be coming straight here."

" Dammit, I do believe it is him. It sure ain't my old man," Jim whispered. " Leave it to me, Enid. I'll 'tend to your father."

" No, no, please don't! Please, don't! " Enid begged. " Jim, please don't lay a hand on him. We don't want to start our married life with a lot of trouble. Let me handle him, Jim."

" I'd sure like to handle him just as I'd like to handle my father."

" But, please, please, don't! Jim, I can handle him. Besides, he's just likely coming to see me."

" He ain't coming to see you alone. He's coming looking for me," Jim whispered. " If you insist, honey, I'll do as you say, though I would like to stay and wring his neck, or kick the seat of his pants back to town."

" No, no! Please go, Jim, please go."

He slid back to the porch, rolled over and got to all fours, then with left hand he patted the porch several times like a dog happily wagging his tail.

That amazing sound brought Lottie out of a doze. Why, shucks, the Edwards family didn't even have a dog.

Lottie sprang to the door, opened it just in time to see a large, very clumsy quadruped high-tailing it along the porch toward the fence. So that was it, was it? Had they had a quarrel, and had Enid made him flee with his tail between his hind legs?

"Lottie, come here, quick! Quick!" Enid whispered. "Pull the door shut."

In a flash Lottie knew that there hadn't been a quarrel, but that there was certain danger. Risking a fall in the dark, she clumped herself down beside the other girl, and as she laid a long, slender arm about Enid's shoulders, she saw what Enid was staring at. There was a man purposefully approaching the front gate.

"Who is it, Enid, who is it? Is it a tramp hobo from the railroad?"

"No, it isn't!" Enid hissed. "It's that fool father of mine. He would come just when Jim and I were having such a good time. We never had such a good chance before to make love."

"But wasn't it cold?"

"Cold! By God, Lottie, you never get cold if you have hot love made to you. Be quiet, Lottie, he's stopping at the gate."

"But, tell me this," Lottie whispered. "Was that Jim I saw hightailin' like a clumsy dog to the end of the porch? Was that him runnin' away from trouble, Enid?"

"No, it wasn't!" Enid hissed, wanting to yell. "He wasn't hightailing it away from trouble. I made him go. I didn't want him and my father getting into a fight after Jim and I'd had such a lovely night."

"Enid, are you sure that's your father there at the gate?"

No time was left for Enid to reaffirm what she'd said, because just then across the intervening forty or fifty feet came this:

"Enid, is that you asettin' there on the edge of that porch with that damned young Villard? If it is, tell the young scoundrel to come out here. I want to talk to him."

"Why, is that you, Dad?" Enid called innocently.

" I thought you were in bed at the Empire Hotel hours ago."

" Yes, I was," Wallace roared. " That's why I ain't asleep now. I got to thinkin' about you and that scamp of a Villard. Send him out here, I want to wring his neck."

" But, Dad, Jim Villard isn't here. He hasn't been here."

" If he ain't, then who the hell's that there beside you, Enid? That's a man! I know it by the cut of his jib."

" And I don't like that a bit! " snapped Lottie Edwards. " Calling me a man. Enid and I were just sitting here having a friendly talk before we went to bed. Here's how it was, Mr. Wallace, we ate so much we felt we couldn't go to bed just now, so a while ago we came out here in the cool air to talk."

" I don't believe a word of this," Bill Wallace growled as he opened the gate. " My eyes are still good, and I saw a man, and I got a hunch I saw Lottie come out of the house."

Wallace was fumbling for a match, when out of the doorway Blacksmith Edwards' bull-like voice roared:

" Who the hell's makin' all this racket out here in front of my house at this time of night? It sounds like a squallin' dogfight with seven cats thrown in! Who knocked a hole in the fence so all the dogs and cats could gather for a council on my front porch? I want to know that! "

" But Papa, Papa," Lottie cried out, almost choking on the desire to laugh. " It's just Mr. Bill Wallace. He's making all the noise."

" Just Bill Wallace! Just Bill Wallace! " the big blacksmith roared. " What's that fightin' old fool of a varmint doin' in my front yard at this time of night? Just keep him there till I get my shotgun! I'll learn him to wake me up out of a snorin' sleep just when I sure needed rest! Don't let the old fool get away, Lottie, and set on that girl if she tries to help him."

" I'm not going to try to help him, Mr. Edwards,"
said Enid. " Dad, you better be hightailin' it, because I
happen to know Mr. Edwards does keep a loaded double-
barrelled shotgun in his bedroom. Dad, please hurry! "

CHAPTER ELEVEN

GEORGE VILLARD had a dream—or rather, two dreams,
one superimposed upon the other. He woke, sitting up
in bed, shivering until his teeth rattled. His eyes bugged
to such an extent that they could have been cut off with
a knife as he stared wildly at the dark walls of his hotel
bedroom. His mouth, which he was unable to shut,
seemed rigid, as rigid as his tongue that protruded from
the middle of the opening. For him, hard shelled as he
was, he was certainly in a strange atmosphere. Had he
dreamed, or had it been something he'd seen in fact.
He, George Villard, of the great Circle 22 outfit, had
actually seen his beloved son married to that worthless
Enid Wallace, and in, of all places, a great corral packed
with milling cattle.

Had that been all, he could have decided that it was a
dream, but it was not all. He could still see Jim astride a
big steer and next to him, that worthless Wallace girl
riding side-saddle on another, while facing these two
animals was a huge spotted steer, with a horn spread of
no less than eight feet, and astride this huge steer was
Jonathan Jones, diminutive, but tremendously whiskered
Big Sage Justice of the Peace. To make the dream more
terrifying, the civil marriage service which Judge Jones
read was as wide as the horns of the steer, seeming to be
thick, white cardboard, with black letters on it.

" Jim Villard," said the judge in a voice as loud as a
locomotive whistle, " do you take this here gal to be your
legally wedded wife, to have and to hold, through sickness
and through health, for better or worse, though I do say

off the record, in my opinion, young man, you're gettin'
a hell of a sight the best of the bargain."

" I do, Judge! " Jim responded, in a voice his shivering
father could still hear.

Then, twisting a little on the back of the spotted steer,
the Justice of the Peace gravely faced Enid Wallace, on
her wild steer, which strangely stood stock still, while all
the other cattle in the corral milled happily round and
round.

" Gal, do you take this here man to be your legally
wedded husband? " Justice of the Peace Jones bellowed,
" for better or worse and so forth? "

" Yes, sir, I do," Enid responded in a voice so shrilly
happy that it seemed to puncture George Villard's ear
drums.

Then the setting changed. They were being married in
Blacksmith Edwards' front yard because the big front
room of the house was not large enough to hold all
the spectators. The contracting parties stood in front
of Reverend Henry Hobson, of the big Methodist
Church.

To the horror of the shivering George Villard, the
ceremony was finished and Reverend Hobson said, his
voice now no louder than the bellow of an old steer:

" Amen. Now, my beloved young people, I, in the
name of God, the Holy Spirit, and the Divine Trinity,
pronounce you man and wife. James, kiss her."

It was when their lips met in a long, clinging caress,
that ended in a loud smack, that Villard discovered that
it had been only a dream. He added a muttered curse,
forgetting all about taking the name of the Deity in vain.
He flung the bed covers over the footrail, sprang out and
began searching for his clothes, still shaking, not from
the cold because he was burning up with rage. He
managed to find a match and lit the kerosene lamp.

" Dratted ingrate, flesh of my flesh! Dratted villain!
Tarnation drat it! " he swore as he got into his thread-
bare store suit.

Though he realised now that he had been dreaming, it had, in his opinion, come to him not wholly as a dream, but as a warning that if he did not hurry, his ungrateful son and that beautiful but worthless Wallace girl would mighty soon be man and wife!

One half of that dream he could put aside as having been sent to him by supernatural channels. It was absurd that the marriage ceremony was about to be performed in a corral full of wild cattle with the coming bride and the coming groom riding a pair of big steers.

As certain as he was of his own identity Villard believed that if he ran he could reach the Edwards' home in time to check that marriage ceremony with something like this:

" By drat, I object to the continuation of this ceremony, Jones! Here are my grounds. That worthless, no-account slut of an Enid Wallace ain't fit to be a life helpmate for my fine, upstandin', honourable son! Stop talkin', Jones."

Getting on his clothes, Villard frantically drew on his boots but without putting on any socks. He found his hat, rammed it down over his close-fitting ears about which iron-grey hair crinkled.

Forgetting the lamp, Villard grabbed the door knob, jerked open the door. For conservative reasons, he chose the back stairway. Finding a match, he struck it on the sole of a boot, almost stumbling over sidewise in the process. As the sulphur sizzled off he saw lying in the yard a handle off a broken garden rake.

" By drat, they could use that rake effectively right here," he muttered righteously. " It's a foul place, indeed! "

He grabbed the rake as though it had been put within reach of his hand by providence. He was in the dark alley, trotting westward. At first he carried the rake handle over his shoulder, but once free of the alley he caught it by one hand and began to swing it angrily, picturing what he was going to do to his vile, sneaking enemies when he reached the Edwards' front yard. He muttered self-righteously, as he trotted southward:

"I'll lambast 'em all, and, by tarnation, I'll larrup that fool son of mine. Ain't whipped him since he was about fourteen, and then with a quirt. This'll do as well as a quirt, especially when it comes to breakin' a few of those villainous, traitorous heads! I'll poke that schemin' slut of a Wallace girl in the belly—her with her sweet, treacherous smile and her plump young breasts! By drat, she's seduced my son, but I'll arrive on time to stop complete seduction!"

At this time all but about thirty or forty of the steers were lying down, peacefully chewing cuds of partially digested wild hay. About the herd would-be young cowboys rode, monotonously singing their chant, this because the six, who had been enthusiasts before dark, had lost their enthusiasm, after they had gone home, filled their stomachs with hot food and hot drink.

A few of the cattle ceased chewing, looked to westward as a strange rattly noise came to them from that direction, a noise which any man would have known was caused by a long, fast-travelling eastbound freight train.

The head of this monster, a dull black thing with a glaring yellow eye, was not more than a quarter-mile away when a big spotted steer heaved himself to his hind feet and with jerky, clumsy motions got his four feet under him.

It might not have been a stampede, only the restless shifting of cattle, had not the voice of that one-eyed monster sounded in a long, doleful, but peremptory wail, for the dropping of the semaphore at the Big Sage depot.

In answer to that scream, the big spotted steer uttered a frightened, panicky bawl that seemed ten yards long and got into motion utterly unconscious of the peace and safety of the other cattle that lay between him and safety to northward.

By the time the second, long-drawn wail of the locomotive began to sound Old Spot was travelling, and behind him a hundred other cattle were travelling, all in the same direction, bawling, clashing horns, breaking down sagebrush. Then by the time the locomotive uttered two short toots acknowledging the dropping of the board, all the cattle except perhaps twenty or thirty, and these were getting to their feet, were travelling fast to north-ward, where some minutes later the frightened leaders were to be brought up by a five-strand barbed wire fence, that protected the wide hayland along the river.

Without thinking that he might latch the Edwards' gate, Bill Wallace fled with one purpose uppermost in his frightened, angry mind, that was to get out of range of Blacksmith Edwards' shotgun in as short as possible a time.

"Damn that red-whiskered Edwards!" he panted as he ran. "I know he's got a hot temper and there ain't no tellin' what he will do when he's all het up about nothin'. Wouldn't be a bit surprised if he lets go both barrels at anything he can see. I didn't mean to wake him up, just wanted to pay Enid a nice, fatherly visit."

It was Enid who grabbed the double barrels of the shot-gun when the irate blacksmith in a long, white night-shirt dashed through the doorway just in time to be grabbed by his frantic and frightened daughter.

While the girls were wrestling with the shotgun and its holder, its holder profanely demanded to be told the location of that noisy son-of-a-bitch so he could be shot. What did he mean making as much noise as a corral full of hungry cattle in the middle of the night?

"But Mr. Edwards, Mr. Edwards!" Enid panted, getting possession of the shotgun. "It's just my father, Bill Wallace. He just came to see me."

"Dad, don't make a fool of yourself," his daughter panted. "Get back into the house. It was just Mr. Wallace come to see Enid."

"All right, all right!" shouted Edwards. "If that's the

case, what did he do with Jim Villard, who was right here courtin' you, Enid? You and him woke me up seven times with your cooin' and billin' and lovemakin'."

"We didn't do anything of the kind, Mr. Edwards," Enid denied and felt her face burn. "We were just sitting here talking—talking about several things."

"All right! All right! Let's say that's all," Edwards roared, "but what becomes of Jim Villard? What did Bill Wallace do to him? It's common knowledge that Bill's goin' to slay young Villard the next time he gets a chance if he don't stay away from you, Enid."

"Papa, shut up! Please shut up!" Lottie begged, still trying to push him into the house. "You're making so much noise every neighbour in town will be here to see what's happening. I don't know what became of Jim Villard except that we made Mr. Wallace think he hadn't been here."

"Damn it, all right! All right! All right!" Edwards bellowed. "But what becomes of Jim Villard? He's here and I know it. Enid, did your pa knife him like he threatened to do?"

"Oh, no, of course he didn't, Mr. Edwards," Enid said as though the blacksmith were totally deaf. "Yes, Jim was here but he got away."

"Did the young varmint turn tail and run?" Edwards demanded in a slightly lowering of voice. "Is that what he turned out to be—a durned cowardly skunk?"

"No, he didn't, Mr. Edwards! No, he didn't!" Enid shouted. "He didn't want to go, but I made him go. He went because he loved me. I didn't want to start our married life by my father killin' him."

"My God, girl," Edwards said and groaned. "Girl, you couldn't marry a dead man. What became of Bill Wallace?"

"Papa, he ran too," Lottie said and tittered. "He turned tail and ran when he heard you were going after your shotgun. He's uptown by this time. He was just hittin' the high places. Isn't that so, Enid?"

"Yes, yes, it is," Enid said and giggled, though she did want to cry.

By this time Bill Wallace had heard enough to stop him in his tracks. He certainly had ample proof that Jim Villard, the damned, sneaky young skunk, had been there at the Edwards', and that he had been aided in his cowardly escape by those two fool, scheming girls. Well, by God, he would go back and settle it with those girls, especially with his own daughter. He was actually turning when he stopped again because through the hundred yards or so of darkness came this, in a recognised bellow of Blacksmith Edwards:

"Bill Wallace, you made more noise than that whole bunch of cattle you shipped yesterday at the shipping pens. You come back and I'll let you have a double charge of buckshot and bore a hole through you you could stick a wagon tongue through! Come on back here, you old fool, wakin' me at this time of night!"

"Damned fool, he ain't got no sense!" said Bill Wallace. "I ain't goin' back there because he's just crazy enough to shoot me. I'll find that Jim Villard to-morrow mornin' and settle with him, and then I'll turn that daughter of mine over my knee and paddle her like I did up to a few years ago—her gettin' stuck on the son of Villainous Villard. By God, I won't tolerate it any longer!"

Convinced that the most sensible thing to do was to return to the hotel and go to bed, Wallace struck off in that direction. He was still panting from his run, a little from fright, but this panting was not sufficient to keep him from seeing a whitish blur on the ground a little way ahead.

He was so angry, however, and sufficiently suffering from frustration to make it impossible for him to decide that that whitish blur was anything more formidable than a little patch of snow.

He most certainly failed to even imagine that a little way beyond the edge of that whitish blur, George Villard was travelling hurriedly toward him brandishing a hard-wood rake handle.

He was about to kick the whitish patch of snow when the whole patch erupted all around him, half smothering him in waving sheets and uttering doleful, menacing, threatening noises that would shake a man's soul to the quick.

The harder Bill Wallace fought, and he fought now only for freedom and free air, the more he was smothered by these sheet-waving ghosts, and the more menacing their doleful howls sounded, telling him he was doomed to eternal hell fire because he had so unjustly mistreated his own daughter and George Villard.

" By God, I didn't ever mistreat that son-of-a-bitch of a Villard! " Wallace panted, trying to break free. " That ornery old thievin' cattle thief—he never did anything but try to mistreat me! "

Seeing that upheaval of white in front of him, George Villard, the rich owner of the Circle 22, in his tense state of mind had only one interpretation to place upon it. It was part of the aftermath celebration of the wedding of his son to that dratted tarnation of a Wallace girl.

In that state of mind, Villard started to wade right into that fighting, churning mass with his rake handle. He was immediately smothered by three sheet-waving figures, one of which hopped on his back, but could not bear him down because just then Mr. Villard, so thoroughly frightened that he had seventeen times his normal strength, threw off his ghostly attacker and got to going well before any of the other ghosts could hop upon his back.

As fast as his middle-aged legs could carry him, he was headed toward the alley from which he could gain the back stairs of the Astor House.

" Dammit to hell! Dammit to hell! " Gimpy shouted, and then snickered. " The stingy old son-of-a-gun got away with my sheet! See it wavin' about his shoulders. Let me after him! Let me after him!"

"Shut up, you idiot!" Hap Lawson hissed. "Ain't you got brains enough to know ghosts can't yell?"

"But dammit, I ain't a ghost, Hap," Gimpy panted, trying to break free from his two captors. "That there was a good sheet. I meant to take it home to Maw."

"Shut up, you damned idiot!" hissed Johnny Granger. "Your mouth is made to eat and drink through, not to yell through. Let's get back and see how the other ghosts are farin' with Bill Wallace."

But the other ghosts were not faring with Bill Wallace, rich owner of the Double W. Mr. Wallace had broken free and at top speed was fleeing to eastward in the blackness, taking any path at seemed an open road. He ran out of wind and leg motion only when deep in the sagebrush about three-eighths of a mile to east of town. He sank limply to his knees, rolled to one side and rested on his shaking elbow.

After resting for perhaps fifteen minutes and trying to think rationally, something he failed to accomplish, he staggered to his feet and set off by a circuitous route for the back yard of the Empire Hotel.

Only after he sat shaking on the edge of his bed for perhaps ten minutes, did George Villard discover what he had brought with him from that hair-raising, soul-shivering experience. He had brought a new bed-sheet. Dropping to his knees, Villard pulled his battered valise from under the bed, opened it. Into it he crammed the bed-sheet. He would take that home to his work-worn, worry-ridden wife. She could use a new bed-sheet, which incidentally would save him the price of one.

Bill Wallace gained the littered back yard of the Empire Hotel, then the rear hall and his bedroom, but not noiselessly. He stumbled over everything in his path, even a bucket and mop and broom in the rear hall.

He gained the safety of his own room and had barely time to light the kerosene lamp when a rap sounded upon the door.

" Anything wrong in there, Bill? I heard you makin' a noise."

" Is that you, Hitch? " Wallace demanded, trying to keep his voice steady.

"Yes, it's me, Bill," said Hitchcock, operator of the hotel, trying the door and finding it locked. " Anything wrong in there? "

" Tell you what you can do, Hitch," said Wallace. " I got an awful case of the gripes, can you find a little likker and fetch it to me? This is the awfullest case of cramps I ever had in my whole life."

" All right," Hitchcock agreed. " I'll bring you a bottle in about three minutes."

Wallace rose unsteadily, blew out the lamp. He managed to unlock the door. He would take the bottle from the accommodating Hitchcock and drink it, though he would certainly not allow himself to be seen.

In the short sagebrush at the southerly edge of Big Sage, ten cowboys were in conference about what was to be done with the ten sheets, when Gimpy, in no uncertain words, said that old son-of-a-gun of a Villard had got away with his sheet, so there were only nine.

" Now, I can just tell you what to do with all nine of them, boys," Gimpy squeaked. " Give 'em to me and I'll take 'em home to Maw. We ain't had a whole sheet in our house for two years. Ma's patched and patched 'em till they're nothin' but patches."

Nine voices promptly vetoed that beseeching suggestion, explaining that Gimpy's mother didn't get any of their new sheets.

" Now, here's what I suggest," argued Tom Jones. " We'll light up a little fire here and as I've got a pencil, we'll scribe on them, and then bundle 'em up and one of us'll sneak back and toss 'em into the Edwards' front yard as a weddin' present for Miss Enid Wallace, who is a damned nice girl, regardless of what any son-of-a-bitch says about her, and the prettiest thing that ever walked on two legs."

"But we can't sign our names on the sheets," suggested Hap Lawson. "That'd give the whole ghost business away. We can't afford to do that."

"We won't sign our names to 'em at all," said Jones. "We'll just write on 'em to Mrs. Enid Villard from a bunch of her admirin' and lovin' friends. Don't you think that should do?"

"Now," offered Johnny Granger, when the last sheet had been inscribed, "what we most need is a bottle."

Then rose the question of who was going to take the untidy bundle of dirty, new bed-sheets to the Edwards' front yard.

"Oh, sure, Gimp'll take 'em," offered Johnny Granger. "Gimp's the best taker in the whole outfit."

"Gimp, he sure won't take 'em, and that's the word with the bark on it," squealed Gimpy. "I'm goin' home, and don't one of you talk back to me, because if you do I might decide to go to old Villainous Villard and suggest that for a price of about five dollars to tell him who robbed him of fifty."

"I was just goin' to say, boys," Tom Jones said grandly, "as how I'd take 'em myself. I'll throw 'em over the fence into the Edwards' front yard and likely somebody'll find 'em in the mornin'. You fellows wait here."

CHAPTER TWELVE

THE SUN rose, without a trace of clouds in the sky. Through the crisp air the detached mountain ranges in every direction came in so close that they threatened to come closer.

There had been so many unusual occurrences during the previous day, so much excitement, so much fighting that Big Sage felt vaguely as if it, as a whole, had been on a drunk.

Johnny Granger and Tom Jones, both flat broke, met in front of the Club Saloon and grinned sheepishly at each other.

" Do you think we could work the barkeep in here out of a pair of drinks? " queried Jones.

" By gosh, I sure pray we can," Johnny groaned. " Me, I'm a sick man."

They got their free drinks, came out and let the sun warm them outside, the whisky doing it fairly well inside. They were beginning to discuss events of the previous night when across the street Bill Wallace shuffled out of the Empire Hotel, stood as if undecided.

" Now, there's a miracle, Tom," said Johnny Granger. "The way he was travellin' away from that bunch of ghosts last night, I figured he was in Utah by this time. Don't he look to you like he'd been run about forty miles durin' the night? "

" Well, he does sag a little at the corners, doesn't he? " Tom said solemnly.

These two cowboys shouted, lifted friendly hands to the owner of the Double W. He stared as though he hardly saw them, lifted a hand half way in return salutation, let it drop.

Wallace turned and made as if to shuffle into the hotel, changed his mind, looked in the direction of the Dodge Brothers' store, which was just opening. He was starting to slant off across to the Dodge store when Tom and Johnny, just by looking at each other, decided they'd get a loan of a few dollars from Bill Wallace.

They intercepted him about the middle of the wide, dusty street and told him he looked just fine, that they had had hard luck last night. They asked him whether he could loan them three more dollars.

" Why, yes, boys," Wallace said in a dazed manner. " Let me see, don't I owe you boys a few dollars? There were so many riders down there in that mix-up I couldn't keep track of all of them, but seems to me you two was there."

H

" Yes, we lent a hand, Bill," Johnny Granger said as if a little doubtful. " Fact is, we tried out best."

" Which wasn't much, Mr. Wallace," Tom said apologetically.

They got four silver dollars, thanked him almost tearfully, told him again that he looked in excellent health. As they turned to go back to their sentry posts in front of the Club Saloon, they grinned shamefacedly at each other.

" Now, that was sure a lowdown dirty trick to play on him," Jones said weakly. " Last night we scared the pants off him and this mornin' we borrow money from him."

" That don't look so lowdown after all," Johnny disagreed. " You can tell by the way he dug up, he don't even suspect that you and me was ghosts, Tom. I didn't know a man of his age and build could run as fast as he can."

" What'll we do, Johnny, go in and get another round of drinks? "

" Now, let me consider that fully. My belly's yellin' at me that it needs grub, and my fingers in my overall pocket tell me I got two dollars. From a strictly financial standpoint, cowboy, let's go to the Chinaman's and get breakfast and then come back here. Have you seen anything of the rest of the spectres? "

" Well, yonder's one of 'em all right," Tom chuckled as he saw Gimpy backing up from where he'd been about to enter the Dodge store in order that Bill Wallace could go in first. " He don't look very ghostly, does he? What you reckon he's goin' to the store so early for? "

" Oh, that's an easy one to answer. Reckon his mama sent him there for some sugar so she can make a sugar tit for him so he can suck it while she's cookin' his breakfast. Let's hightail it, if he sees us, he'll want us to buy him a drink."

Though the bundle of sheets had not yet been found in the Edwards' front yard, Mrs. Edwards, from where she was getting breakfast in the kitchen, had a fair view of the back yard. Not satified with what her eyes told her, she bustled into the back yard and counted the dry garments on the clothes-line. Then she bustled angrily into the house and toward the bedroom where Enid Wallace and her own daughter were giggling, being awake but not yet up. She swung open the door and demanded that they tell her what had become of that sixth sheet which rightfully should have been on the clothes-line. Before the girls could answer, she went on, and angrily:

"You needn't be so high-toned and finicky just because you got girl company, Lottie. You changed the sheet on that bed yesterday. Lottie, what becomes of that sheet? I mean the one you took off this bed?"

The girls protested in a convincing manner that they hadn't disturbed the sheets on the bed. Most certainly they had not taken one from the clothes-line.

"Well, I reckon maybe you're right," Mrs. Edwards said without conviction. "Perhaps I didn't wash up as many as I figured I had. As long as you girls are awake, you'd just as well get up and help me with breakfast and set the table."

"We'll be up in just a minute, Mama," Lottie promised as her mother bustled out. "Now, what do you suppose become of that bed-sheet? I know there were nine on the line yesterday evening, because I hung them there myself. Do you suppose——"

"Well, I really don't know," Enid said. "But I do know this much, Lottie, when we rushed out last night on hearin' all that racket and seein' all that white stuff out there, I'll swear we counted ten travellin' sheets after somebody. Until I discovered that those sheets were wrapped around men, I was most scared to death."

"Well," Lottie said and laughed, "I wonder who that was they were chasin'? Have you got any notion about it?"

"No, Lottie, I haven't, but I sure hope it was my bull-headed old father. Do you suppose Jim Villard, as he ran around the house, could have grabbed that sheet off the clothes-line just to be ready to smother somebody in it? "

They were dressed and in the kitchen, offering to do anything for Mrs. Edwards, when in lumbered the blacksmith from the front door with a dirty, straggly-tied bundle in his arms, which he dumped to the floor with the announcement that he'd found it in his own front yard. What was the meaning of it? Was it somebody's damned fool way of thinking they were funny, or was there an abandoned baby in it?

" Abandoned infant? Abandoned infant? " gasped Mrs. Edwards and puckered her face. " Why, I don't know any girl in this town who was ready to give birth to an illegal child. Of course, there's talk about Susie Wilkins, but there's usually talk about Susie."

The girls were on their knees now, doing their utmost to be gentle as they unrolled the bundle.

" Oh, gosh, Mama! " Lottie said almost tearfully. " There's no baby in this bundle of sheets. Now I won't have any baby to adopt. I'm so disappointed."

" Get married, and you can find one in less than a year," her hungry father growled. " Who do you suppose dumped that bundle of old dirty sheets in our front yard? "

" Mr. Edwards, these are not old sheets! " Enid said, holding up an armful of them. " They're new sheets! They're just dirty. Wait, look here! There's writing on this one—pencil writing. Wait'll I make it out."

With the three women deciphering and Blacksmith Edwards glowering down upon them, it was soon evident that these nine new, if dirty, sheets had been presented to Enid Wallace and Jim Villard as a wedding present.

" But dammit, dammit," Edwards growled, as if he were not sure of himself. " Enid, you and him aren't married yet, are you, so how in the hell could you get a weddin' present, and such a present as this? "

" Of course they're not married, Edwards," his wife

blazed. " But they're goin' to be. Enid, of course they're
your sheets. I'll wash them all for you just as soon as the
breakfast things are done and you and Lottie can iron
them. It's going to be a fine forenoon for dryin' sheets."

Lottie reminded her mother that Enid and Jim could
not yet use the sheets even if they were freshly laundered.

" Oh, we'll use them all right," Enid corrected softly.
" Don't you worry about that."

" But Enid, honey," Mrs. Edwards begged in a shocked
voice, " you and Jim wouldn't use them sheets without
bein' married, would you? Don't be hurt by answerin'
that question."

" We'll use them all right, Mrs. Edwards," Enid said
after she sprang to her feet. " Mrs. Edwards, do you
care if I put them to soak in that tub on the back porch? "

" That there girl," said the blacksmith as he stroked
his whiskers, " sure wants to get married, don't she? "

" And God grant," his wife said prayerfully, " she don't
do anything wrong before she does get married. Of all
the crazy things I ever heard about—makin' that couple
a weddin' present of nine dirty sheets before they've even
set a date for bein' married. Edwards, set down. I'll
fetch your vittles."

Prompted by curiosity, fear and hope, Gimpy went
close to one of the front windows of the big general store
as soon as Bill Wallace had entered. Without showing
more than half his scrawny self, Gimpy put a big ear to
the glass. He simply had to hear Wallace confess that at
last he had given his consent to the marriage of his
daughter to Jim Villard.

" Good mornin', Bill," Lou Dodge, who made a practice of opening the store, said. " What's wrong with you,
Bill? You must 'a' had too bad a day yesterday."

" Yes, Lou, I did have a bad day yesterday," Wallace
said. " But most of my trouble is caused by a bad night.
Fact is, Lou, I had a hell of a night! It must 'a' been
somethin' I et over there at Hitchcock's damned hotel."

" Yes, likely it was," Dodge sympathised.   " Of

course, if you feel too bad, you'd best look up Doc Lancaster."

"Well, now, I don't believe I'm sick enough to need Doc Lancaster," Wallace muttered. "Here's what may help a little. If you've got a bottle open, I may drink with you."

"Yes, I always keep a bottle open for my customers," Lou Dodge agreed. "Come on back to the office with me and we'll see what we can do to it."

They went to the office, which was at the rear of the big store, in one corner, and there both drank from the neck of a bottle. But being thus stimulated, Wallace could not get the courage to confess that he'd come to talk over his family troubles with Lou Dodge, nor would he admit that he had not gone to the saloon for a drink in fear of meeting one or more of those ghosts of last night. His guess was that they'd all been Villard's men. On top of all his other troubles he didn't want to have to kill a couple of them or be killed by one of them.

"Now, I do feel a little better, Lou," he muttered. "Give me a plug of chewin' tobacco and I'll go back over to Hitch's and get some breakfast."

He got the plug of Star and was about to shuffle out when Lou Dodge said, he being very curious about what had occurred last night:

"Bill, I been told that at last you've given your consent for Enid to marry Jim Villard. Let me congratulate you. It's the only sensible way to look at that business, Bill. Jim's a fine boy, no matter how cussed his father is. Bill, let me shake your hand."

"Keep away from my hand, Lou," Wallace roared as he brandished the plug of tobacco. "Who the hell told you that? Whoever he was he was a damned liar. I'd rather see Enid in her grave than to be the wife of that ornery, no-account son-of-a-bitch of a son of George Villard!"

He rushed out, slapping his leg angrily with the plug of tobacco as he went. But instead of allowing Gimpy

to be the next customer, in rushed Justice of the Peace
Jones, short legs, long whiskers and all.

"Now that damned old varmint," Gimpy muttered.
"I wonder what he wants? He's a hell of a man to be
justice of the peace. He ain't got no manners at all.
Barged right in there in front of me as I was about to
open the door."

"Why, good mornin', Judge," said Lou Dodge. "Are
you feelin' bad too? Judge, you don't look too well.
How about a nip from my store bottle?"

"By God, yes, Lou, lead me to that bottle. That
worthless son of mine emptied mine last night. Didn't
realise he knew where I kept it cached. As you know,
his ma's agin drinkin'."

"I want a full bottle of Harper's and I'll hide it in a
new place," declared the judge. "That worthless son
of mine won't find it, and neither will his ma. When she
finds 'em, she busts 'em, but when Tom finds 'em, he
empties 'em."

Lou Dodge speaking very seriously reminded him that
just a little while ago he had seen Tom down the street
talking to Johnny Granger, that they'd both looked stone
sober.

"Yes, maybe you're right, Lou, maybe you're right.
Don't see how Tom could have drunk it all and not shown
the effects of some of it this mornin', but you can never
tell about him. Maybe he took two or three drinks out of
it and sold the rest to a damned Injun to get a little
poker money. I don't know what I'm goin' to do with
that boy, Lou. He ain't a bad son at heart, but since he's
got to bein' a cowboy, you never can tell what he's goin'
to do next. Charge the bottle, Lou, if you don't mind
till I get my next county cheque. By the way, Lou, there's
a report goin' around to the effect that Bill Wallace, the
damned old fool, has at last consented for his daughter,
Enid, to marry Jim Villard, who's father's a damned old
fool too. Any reliable truth in that?"

"No, not a bit of truth, Judge," Lou Dodge said

soberly. "Bill Wallace was in here just a while ago. When I mentioned the rumour to him, he sure went into the air and came down stiff-legged, tellin' me that he'd rather see Enid in her grave than married to young Villard. Awful wish for a father to have, ain't it?"

"A sinful, deplorable wish," Jones nodded, shaking his venerable head. "No good can come to any man who has such a sinful wish as that, Lou. If Bill Wallace only realised that he can't dodge rightful retribution, he would sooner or later learn, by God, that his chickens come home to roost. Sorry to hurry, Lou; but I got to get home while my wife's workin' in the kitchen and before Tom goes around and sees where I'm goin' to hide my bottle in a new place."

As Judge Jones made his exit, with the quart of whisky poked into a pocket of his trousers, part of the neck of the bottle pushed up his dingy black coat as though he was toting around a young cannon in his hip pocket.

"Mornin', Judge Jones," said Gimpy, suppressing his excitement.

He was about to add something to this when Jones made a noise like the angry grunt of disgusted old boar hog and strode away around the corner, which was the shortest route to his home.

"Now the old son-of-a-bitch needn't snub me like that," Gimpy growled. "What do you suppose he's totin' that big gun in his hip pocket for?"

Gimpy was too happy and hopefully expectant to be angry for long. He opened the door and jingled in, his old sombrero on the back of his curiously-shaped, straw-coloured head.

"Why, good mornin', Gimpy," said Lou Dodge. "What makes you so happy? Bill Wallace and the Judge were sure out of sorts. What can I do to serve the needs of a happy customer?"

"Bet your durned life, I'm happy, Lou," Gimpy agreed and sneered. "I just dropped in to get them twenty-five dollars you owe me. You recollect them twenty-five dollars you were going to pay to me and a few of my friends just to scare old Bill Wallace to death?"

"Yes, but you didn't scare him to death," Lou Dodge reminded sternly. "He was in here a while ago and he sure wasn't a dead man, even if he did look like a sick man. I genuinely regret, Gimpy, that I must remind you that you and your friends didn't earn those twenty-five dollars."

"We didn't? We didn't?" Gimpy stammered, as his face paled. "But he was in here a little while ago. I seen him myself. Wasn't he in here, Lou? Did he confess to you, Lou, his most trusted friend, that he'd give his consent for his girl Enid to marry Jim Villard? Wasn't that what he said, Lou? It seems to me that's what he said when I was out there keepin' my ears glued to the window glass? Did he say somethin' else—somethin' else different than that?"

"Yes, it was quite different than that, Gimpy," Lou Dodge said. "He said he'd rather see Enid in the grave than see her married to Jim Villard. I'm sorry, Gimpy, I can't hand over your twenty-five, as I sure wanted to see that marriage come off, but I reckon we'll even have to quit thinkin' about it. If you want credit for a few dollars, it's all right."

"All right, Lou, all right," Gimpy muttered and groaned and looked at the floor. "Give me ten sacks of Bull Durham and a pound of striped stick candy and about ten packs of brown cigarette paper. I'm leavin' town as soon as I can saddle me a horse and ride."

"But what about your friends, Gimp, your associates of last night?" objected Lou Dodge. "You ain't desertin' them, are you?"

"No, sir, hell, no!" Gimpy corrected, managing a feeble grin. "Here's why I'm goin'. Lou, I'm hittin' the high places before them friends and associates of mine learn what didn't happen. If they learn what didn't happen, they'll cut me up in nine pieces and divide 'em up among themselves. Lou, I'm sorry to be in a hurry, but that's why I'm hittin' the high spots. Give me half an hour's lead, will you? "

" I will," Lou Dodge promised sadly, sorry for this homely cowboy, but sorrier for himself because he had instigated the ghost plot and it had failed.

But had it failed? According to the picture of Bill Wallace the young merchant saw now, something, possibly ghosts, had caused him to have an extremely painful and unrestful night.

" Bad case of gripes and cramps," Lou Dodge soliloquised and chuckled. " The trouble with him is, he got his pants scared off and he hasn't got 'em back on again. Say, this is something I've got to tell brother Frank! "

CHAPTER THIRTEEN

GEORGE VILLARD awoke at daylight, his average time for getting up in order that little escape his supervision or attention. This bright, crisp morning, however, he continued to lie in bed. Here was his reasoning for this breaking of a lifelong rule.

Here in the small room he could be alone with himself and the perfection of his thoughts. Now was the time to do some calm and impartial reasoning. He could not attain this calmness, however, because every time he started to think coolly, he was haunted by that dream of the night. Though he'd been scared out of about seven years of his life by those sheet-wrapped figures, he was convinced now that that prank had been nothing more or less than the celebration of his son's marriage to Enid Wallace.

Drat durn, Bill Wallace! He had schemed and sneaked that marriage over while his old friend, George Villard, had been peacefully and innocently resting in his hotel bedroom. That brand of lowdown justice called for only one thing in reprisal. He, George Villard, would tell Dobie Dick Donovan to lead a small band of riders against the Double W, burning, killing, cutting fences, shooting and stealing cattle until Bill Wallace would be more than happy to hightail it out of Nevada. That was the only sensible manner to deal with such a contemptible ingrate as Wallace.

"Well, I suppose I'll have to put up with the girl," Villard sourly soliloquised. "Her bein' married to my son, I'll have to try my best to treat her impartially, but just the same, I'll cut Jim off with a small part of my fortune because of his dratted ingratitude. I'm more than convinced that this is Bill Wallace's way of trying to get hold of part of my money and range. Now that his daughter is my daughter-in-law he thinks that that will give him a special privilege. Like tarnation it will!"

He found it utterly impossible to keep business from intruding into his family thoughts. There was the matter of nearly a thousand steers, which he had to ship to-day, and there were those forty Double W steers mixed with his beef herd. If Wallace remotely resembled an honourable gentleman he would come and volunteer the information that those forty beef should rightfully be shipped with the Circle 22 cattle, as George Villard's beef.

"But he won't," Villard said bitterly and self-righteously. "No, by tarnation, he won't! If he gave me a hundred of his steers he wouldn't repay me for all the worry and trouble he caused me yesterday, and on top of that with the shame and disgrace of forcing me to brawl with him there in front of the railroad depot. The man is entitled to nothing short of war, and by drat, I'll wage it!"

He had another, and not much smaller, worry—the strange fraternisation of his wagon boss, upon whom for years he had depended, even for killing and stealing, with Wallace's foreman, Brazos Cobb.

What had come over Dobie Dick? Had he some ul-
terior motive for this fraternisation, or had he got religion?
Villard told himself that he could vividly remember the
many times Dobie Dick had said he was going to kill
Brazos Cobb at the first opportunity.

About thirty yards back of the ugly, paintless residence
of Justice of the Peace Jones was a small combined barn
and coal shed. It had a shake roof, while its sides and
front and rear were made of up and down boards with
the cracks battened. The judge, with a well-satisfied
smile on his venerable face, was emerging from this shed,
when he stopped as though he'd run against a heavy
post. There coming around one side of his house was his
tall, good-looking, strapping son, who also looked well-
satisfied with himself. Instantly the judge's gorge rose.
He snarled at his son because he was already too angry
to form a single word.

"Mornin', Judge," drawled Tom. "Been hidin' another bottle? I'm right sorry to have molested your
bottle last night."

Knowing well his wife's hatred for liquor, the judge
crooked a commanding finger at his son.

"Come here, Thomas!" he snarled. "I want you to
listen to a few plain words."

Tom did not come to a halt until he stood about
six feet in front of his irate father, then he said, and
soberly:

"Judge, I meant to sneak a full bottle in there in place
of the one we took last night, but I hadn't got around to
it yet. I've got to congraulate you on the quality of the
whisky you drink."

Much against his will the judge felt himself mollified.
The next moment he was feeling much more charitable
toward Thomas, and the next moment he invited Tom
to go into the shed with him so they could both sample
the contents of the bottle.

"No, I just had breakfast at the Chinaman's restaurant,

Judge," Tom explained. " I don't feel the need of a dram now."

" Well, now, that gratifies me deeply, Thomas," the judge said, waggling his long white whiskers. " You're a more temperate boy than I thought you were. Who the hell was with you here last night? "

The diminutive old judge stood so sober and silent that an onlooker would have thought he was seriously considering how to render a just verdict in court, while he listened to Tom's explanation in which his son admitted that he and nine confederates had forcibly taken fifty dollars away from George Villard.

" Yip! " the judge chuckled loudly. " So you scared the drawers and the underpants offen Bill Wallace and George Villard, eh? "

" Well, we frightened 'em a little, Judge," Tom said very soberly.

" By damn my own pants! " the judge guffawed, slapping his leg. " I'd given my interest in heaven to be witness to that. Which was scared the worst, Thomas? "

" Well, now, Judge, that'd be hard to tell. I guess it was about a draw, but the sad part of it is, our main purpose failed."

" Your purpose? " queried the judge. " What was that? "

Tom confessed that the main purpose of himself and his nine confederates had been the frightening of Bill Wallace to such an extent that the owner of the Double W would willingly consent to the marriage of Enid to Jim Villard.

" Thomas, that was certainly a right noble purpose," the judge said gravely. " Wallace is the orneriest man I ever knowed, even if he is my friend. Did your noble purpose fail, and if so, why? "

" Judge, here's why," Tom said and laughed loudly. " Bill Wallace was scared so he was runnin' so fast all ten of us put together couldn't overtake him. Pap, he was sure hittin' the high places. I didn't know a man of his age could run that fast."

"Well," Judge Jones said, trying to be grave, "you never can tell how fast a man can run till he gets scared by ghosts."

They were now laughing so loudly and with such mutual happiness that they unwittingly brought the judge's wife to the narrow back porch. She was a tall, heavy formidable woman, who, without knowing it, wore dresses that made her look about twice as large as she actually was. She demanded to be told what all the fun was about, explaining that if she liked it, she'd come out and join in the merriment.

"Dammit, Thomas, don't tell her anything," the judge whispered. "If she gets hold of it, it'll be all over town in ten minutes."

"Why, good mornin', Ma," he drawled affectionately. "The judge and I were just laughing about that fight between George Villard and Bill Wallace yesterday in front of the depot. Ma, it was the funniest thing you ever saw, those two old stags tryin' to beat each other to death."

"Oh, is that all?" she said with a sniff. "I heard all about that disgraceful affair from a dozen people. Is that your idea of comedy?"

"Tell her yes," whispered the judge. "I want somebody to side with me once in a while."

"Yes, Ma, it was sort of comical," Tom said emphatically.

"You two come into breakfast," she snapped; "it's waitin'."

"Right away, sweetheart, right away," the judge agreed.

"Sweetheart, sweetheart," she sneered, curling her upper lip.

"We'll be there in just about a minute, Ma. I want to get the judge's advice on a point of law."

That sent her into the kitchen with a heart full of

happiness and motherly affection, even a little affection and respect for her spouse.

"Now, what's that there point of law you want to know about, Thomas?" the judge whispered. "Do you think it's safe for us two to sneak into the shed and get another couple of drams?"

"No, I don't think it would be, Judge," Tom said. "She'd smell it on us and then hell'll pop. You already smell like you'd had a couple. Want a clove, Judge?"

"Hell, no, Thomas! Those act on her like a red flag to a bull. Got anything else?"

"Got some cinnamon bark here somewhere, Judge. I use it when I go callin' on a lady after I take a few drinks."

"Then, hell's fire, give me some cinnamon bark, Tommy, and it won't smell unnatural. Thank you, son. I'll chew on this cinnamon bark and explain that point of law you want good advice about. Ain't been in serious trouble, have you? If you have been, I'll see to it you get out."

Trying to make the question a hypothetical one, and making a mess of it, Tom asked whether ten men had committed a crime if they forcibly took fifty dollars away from a man who actually owed it to them.

"Thomas, who the hell have you and your nine friends been robbin'?" Judge Jones demanded indignantly.

"We didn't rob him, Judge," said Tom. "He owed it to us and we just collected it."

"Who's he?" the judge demanded. "I'll give you my judicial opinion when you tell me his name."

"Hell, Judge, we didn't steal it, we just collected it from George Villard—from old Villainous Villard."

The judge's expression changed immediately.

"Now, you tell me the truth, Thomas," he ordered. "Did you and your nine friends honestly take fifty dollars away from Villard, the stingy old son-of-a-bitch, when he figured he didn't owe it? "

" Judge, we sure did," Tom said and grinned broadly.

" Now, let me consider the evidence produced at this here hearin'," Judge Jones said gravely. " Case dismissed with costs assessed against George Villard. Thomas, why didn't you and your friends make it a hundred. Come on in, now, son, and eat some breakfast with your Ma. It'll make her feel a heap better. If you've got any more cinnamon bark, give her a little of it."

George Villard did not go downstairs until he was certain he would breakfast alone in the dining-room of the Astor House. He found he was without company, but his breakfast was made less enjoyable because upon looking through the front window he could see Bill Wallace talking with Hitchcock in front of the latter's Empire Hotel. They were both Villard's enemies so he imagined as though he could hear them, that they were discussing him and not charitably. He tried to soothe down his feeling by telling himself they were both ignorant ingrates, and beneath his contempt. He would go out the front way to show them they were beneath his sphere.

Villard had barely stepped to the boardwalk when he espied Judge Jones.

" Why, good mornin', Villard," the judge said happily. " What's wrong, George? You look a little to me as if you'd been pulled through a knothole. Feelin' bad? "

" On the contrary, Jones," the owner of the Circle 22 snapped. " I'm feelin' fine—most excellent. I trust you are feeling as well as I do."

" Oh, I'm feelin' bully," the judge chuckled. " What's on your chest, George? By the look on your face, somethin's worryin' you. Anybody been takin' money away from you, George, when you didn't owe it? "

" No, no, nothing of that sort," Villard reassured. " As you know I keep my bills paid promptly. Judge, I been thinkin'. Are you sure I won't take some of your valuable time? "

" Hell, no, I ain't got nothin' special to do. Go ahead! Let her go! You'll feel better when you get it off your chest. I ain't sayin' I can help you out, but I'll do my best. Knowed you weren't feelin' good the minute I set eyes on you. Glad to be of service to you. Won't cost you a cent."

Villard began by saying that he supposed Judge Jones had performed many marriage ceremonies, had he not?

" Yes, sir, quite a number," Jones agreed.

Villard knew that as a hard-headed, conservative cattleman he should not work around to that dream he'd had, but he was powerless to keep away from it.

" And I suppose you married 'em in strange settin's and circumstances, Jones? A man who has been Justice of the Peace as long as you have would likely have some interestin' tales to tell about those ceremonies."

" Yes, sir, I have," Jones said, waving his cigar. " I've performed many a shotgun marriage in my time. You know what a shotgun marriage is, don't you, Villard? That's when it's a trifle hasty due to the pressin' pressure of nature. I've married 'em standin' up and I've married 'em layin' down. I've joined 'em in the holy bonds of matrimony when they was on horseback or muleback, ridin' in buckboards or freight wagons. Villard, have you got time for me to tell you about a marriage ceremony I performed while I was Justice of the Peace in the town of Sonora, California? In all my marryin' experiences I'm dead certain that was the most interestin' ceremony I ever performed. The prospective bride and groom showed up in Sonora well mounted and they agreed to pay me five dollars if I'd join them in holy wedlock while they set their saddles. They ordered me to stand on the ground right in front of their mounts, but I wouldn't do it."

" But didn't you join them in matrimony? " Villard

I

stammered. " You surely didn't overlook the five dollars, Judge? "

" You're damned right I didn't, Villard, but I had my way. If they insisted on remainin' in their saddles, I told them I had to get me a suitable mount too so I could perform the marriage ceremony on horseback."

" Jones, are you sure," muttered Villard, much against his will, " that you didn't get a big spotted steer to ride on when you married those two? "

" Big spotted steer? " the judge accused. " What in the hell are you talkin' about? For that ceremony I got the loan of a big black stallion, which was a fine lookin' horse. I recollect like it was but yesterday as how I rested my marriage ceremony book on the horn of the saddle as I read the legal ceremony to 'em."

Justice of the Peace Jones was preparing to enlarge and embellish that tale, when round the corner came Jim Villard, wearing new overalls and new shirt, and Enid Wallace, extremely pretty in a bright, well-fitting calico dress.

Villard's first reaction was a look of stark incredulity at being openly flaunted in this manner. Then he uttered an enraged snort, followed by:

" Excuse me, Jones, and thank you for the legal advice. I've got a word or two to speak to that son of mine. He's been triflin' around town too much to suit me."

" Tell you the rest of that later, Hitch," snorted Bill Wallace across the street as he saw the apparently happy young couple. " I want that fool girl of mine to tell me what she means by runnin' around with that goddamned Jim Villard in broad daylight! "

He struck out for the promised scene of battle at a clumsy dogtrot and upon seeing his hated enemy coming, Villard swerved to his left and trotted out to meet him, allowing Jim and Enid to stop in what seemed to be an atmosphere of happiness, determination and fear.

" Now what do you suppose is going to happen, Jim? "

Enid whispered. " You won't let it make any difference, will you? "

" Not a damned bit," growled Jim Villard. " Let 'em fight it out—kill each other if they're dead set on it. No, honey, it won't make any difference."

The would-be gladiators, who were rich ranchers, were perhaps sixty feet apart when Hitchcock shouted:

" Hey! Put that off a few minutes, you two! Villard, here comes Dave Brookins, your straw boss at your river ranch, in a buckboard like he's lookin' for you."

The next moment a span of sweaty mustangs, followed by a bouncing buckboard, rounded the end of the depot and headed eastward on the main street. The driver, a tall, fat man, made the right side of the buckboard seat sag as he lashed the mustangs with a stubby whip.

" Wait a minute, Wallace," Villard shouted. " I'll tend to your wants later. I want to see what news Dave Brookins is bringin' to me. What brings you to town this time of the mornin' without my order, Brookins? "

" What fetches me to town without your order, Villard? " Brookins cursed. " I'm here to find out what you mean by lettin' about a thousand head of your beef in my hay fields when I ain't got the stacks fenced yet? What do you mean by that? "

" My beef herd is in my own river hay fields and the stacks ain't fenced yet? " Villard croaked and looked blank. " Why, my beef herd was out there in the sage-brush beyond the shippin' pens the last I heard of it. I was goin' to ship it to-day."

" Well, by God, it's not there now! " Brookins cursed. " When we got up down at the Circle 22 this mornin' there was the whole damned beef herd lined up outside the barbed wire fence bawlin' to be let in and not a solitary rider with 'em. Villard, that's a hell of a way to treat your beef cattle. Not knowin' what else to do, I rode out there with a couple of men and let 'em in. What kind of a cowman are you anyway, Villard? "

"And I want to know, Brookins," roared Bill Wallace, "are there about forty of my beef in that herd?"

"Why, good mornin', Bill," said the strawboss of the Circle 22. "How are you, anyway, Bill? Yeah, there is a little of your stuff in with that herd—thirty or forty, maybe."

CHAPTER FOURTEEN

ONCE VILLARD realised that his beef herd were at the big hay ranch ten miles down the river instead of being ready for loading at the shipping pens, he flung up his hands in anger and horror, and groaned in self-commiseration. As he looked about for somebody to blame, his fierce eyes fell upon his son Jim.

"Drat it, son!" he roared. "Why didn't you put a night herd on those cattle instead of spendin' your time with that wench?"

Jim whispered something to the suddenly pale girl and stepped forward. He stopped.

"Dad, that'll be enough such talk from you," he said softly as a grey line appeared around his mouth. "Say what you want about me but not another word from you about Enid!"

"By God," Bill Wallace ejaculated under his breath. "He's got better stuff in him than I figured he had. I was going to lay Enid across my knee and paddle her hard for runnin' around with him, but now I'll wait for a while."

"Well," Villard demanded without apparent concession, "Jim, why in tarnation didn't you put a night guard on those cattle?"

"Why didn't you?" Jim retorted. "I'm not bossin' the Circle 22 outfit, am I? I'll answer that for you. You think I'm not cowman enough to run an outfit like that. Maybe I'm not. Where's your prize pet, Dobie Dick?"

At that moment Dobie Dick Donovan and Brazos Cobb came out of the Club Saloon, arm in arm and apparently extremely happy, though each did wear his big, holstered six-shooter.

" There's your wagon boss," said Jim as he stepped back to Enid's side. " Ask him why he didn't put night herders on those beef."

" What's this? What's this? " growled Dobie Dick, his beard-stubbled face becoming sullen. " Who's talkin' about my way of runnin' the Circle 22? Why, good mornin', young lady! You're sure lookin' beautiful this fine mornin'."

" Good mornin', Dobie," Enid whispered through colourless lips.

" Well, good mornin', sweetheart," said the ugly, diminutive Brazos Cobb, grinning happily. " Ain't feelin' bad, are you? Sure hope not."

" I'm all right, Brazos," she murmured.

Villard, mad enough to jump up and down and scream, had difficulty finding the words he wanted to use without profaning the name of the Deity. This silence gave Brookins time to explain the situation. Dobie Dick Donovan grinned broadly, shrugged and said:

" It wasn't my business last night to put a night guard on them steers. Me and Brazos here were takin' us a vacation. I don't see that any hell of a lot of damage is done, anyway. How'd they come to get down there, anyway, Brookins, or can you read sign? They wasn't driv down there on purpose by somebody, was they? "

" Most dratted certain they were! " Villard roared and started to search for his hated enemy. " You, Wallace, you dratted scoundrel, you're responsible for them beef cattle of mine bein' down at my home ranch instead of where I can load 'em right away! "

" And Villard, you're a dirty damned liar! " growled Bill Wallace, as he reached for right hip pocket which was empty.

" Now, no shootin' here, you two little boys," warned

Sheriff Andy Smith, who had appeared at a trot. " Go to it and fight it out if you won't be satisfied with any-thing else. I'll referee the match."

Villard whirled upon him, telling him that he had better tend to his business as sheriff·instead of refereein' a brawl.

" I'll brawl with the crazy old stag if he's bent on doin' that," Wallace challenged. " I've thought for a long time that nothin' would put more sense into his fool head than a first-class lickin'. Come on, Villard. Here's a good crowd to watch me whale the hell out of you! "

Just when it looked as though the two rich ranchers were going to rush each other, with the growing crowd as happy audience and the sheriff as referee, somebody bawled like a sick cow:

" Oh, hell, them two stags can't put up a fight! I'm plumb disgusted. Why don't you put 'em both in jail so this town can have a peaceable existence."

" I will if they don't behave themselves," growled the sheriff. " Since they arrived yesterday with their beef herds, there's been more trouble in Big Sage than there's been in the past year."

Just then Johnny Granger arrived at an unsteady lope shouting, " Let 'em go to it! Let 'em go to it! Villard there, he's got plenty to be mad about. Ten travelling hoboes robbed him of fifty dollars last night. Ain't he told everybody about it? "

" No, tarnation, I haven't! " Villard exploded weakly. " I'm not a man to tell my troubles. I'm man enough to keep my troubles to myself."

" Say, Villard, why didn't you tell me about that? " the sheriff immediately demanded. " I might have been able to recover at least part of your money. There were ten of 'em? "

" I don't know! " Villard growled, looking at the ground. " As I just said, I keep my troubles to myself."

" Now listen to what he says! " Bill Wallace taunted. " As we all know he's a hell of a trouble maker, but the hell of it is he wants to tell the world about it. Ain't that so, Dobie Dick, you should know?"

"Oh, yes, that's about right," drawled Dobie Dick, who was about half drunk. "Most of the time he's a damned nuisance, but as he thinks he is so smart and he pays me good wages, I listen to him. I ain't in a listenin' mood to-day, as Brazos and me, we're takin' us a vacation. Ain't that right, Brazos?"

"That's plumb right, Dobie," said the other gunman with such an enthusiastic voice that Enid had to clutch Jim's arm. "Yes, sir, we're takin' us a plumb vacation."

"Jim, there's going to be trouble between those two," Enid whispered, clutching his arm more tightly. "It's not like such a pair as they are to stay friendly very long."

Villard, again in full voice, was insulting Bill Wallace and telling him what a skunk he was, and Wallace, never out of voice, was more than matching the accusations and contempt offered by the owner of the Circle 22.

"Damn you two," the sheriff barked. "If you don't quit your growlin' and get to fightin', I'll put you both in jail. You've kept this town off balance ever since you hit here with your beef herds yesterday. I'm plumb tired of you two."

"You'd imprison me, Smith?" Villard said as he turned upon the sheriff. "Have you forgot that I'm a member of the Board of County Commissioners and have influence?"

"Yes, you've got influence, but you've got damned little sense, Villard," the sheriff sneered. "I think a lot of people are wonderin' why they ever elected you to the Board of Commissioners."

"I ain't wonderin' about that," Bill Wallace chuckled. "I never voted for him."

That started Villard off on a stern lecture, the subject of which was his reminding these people of what a righteous man he was. The sheriff checked him with:

"You needn't tell 'em, George, they all know."

Jim and Enid were actually beginning to enjoy all of this squabbling, which seemed to threaten no bloodshed, when the girl uttered a gasp and whispered:

"Jim, there's Judge Jones now! Shall we talk to him now?"

Before the handsome son of George Villard could answer that, a voice slightly hoarse with a breath of whisky whispered in his near ear:

"Don't bother the judge as he's enjoyin' himself. I'm the judge's son. Tell me what you want."

"Damn you, Tom!" Jim Villard snarled as he whirled. "Don't you blow your whisky breath in my ear again. I've got a notion to slug you!"

"No, no, Jimmy, you wouldn't slug me," Tom corrected confidently. "Not when there's a handsome young lady like Enid present. Maybe you didn't know it, Jim, but Enid there she once most loved me. Ain't that plumb correct, Enid?"

"No, I didn't!" Enid snorted, but blushed furiously. "It's not so!"

Villard declared that he was going to leave his beef herd on the hay land for a few days to let them regain the weight they had lost.

"Ain't you forgettin' about shippin' regulations?" drawled Brazos Cobb.

"Shippin' regulations? Shippin' regulations?" Villard demanded, turning to see who had addressed him. "You little misshapen misfit, this doesn't concern you. If Wallace over there won't keep silent, maybe you will."

"I will, Mr. Villard!" Wallace agreed and grinned happily. "Just as soon as I tell you that keepin' those beef down there at the hay ranch will cost you about eighty dollars a day."

"Eighty dollars a day!" Villard demanded. "Why will postponing shipping my beef for a few days cost me eighty dollars a day. Those are my forty empty cars on the shipping pen spur, and I can ship my own beef cattle whenever I want to ship 'em!"

" Whoopee! " exalted Bill Wallace. " By gosh, he is losin' his memory. That's a sign he's goin' all to pieces. He's forgot that the railroad will charge him two dollars a day demurrage for every day he holds them cattle cars."

There was such a clamour now, that Jim barely heard Enid as she demanded to be told whether that were correct.

" Yes, that's true, honey," Jim said, putting his lips close to her ear. " Look at the hurt and righteousness on the old man's face, Enid. He's figurin' out already that the railroad company's robbin' him. There he goes."

" But where is he going? " she demanded. " I'm not tall enough to see over the heads of all the other people."

" He's hightailin' it for the railroad depot," said Tom Jones. " It beats all hell, don't it, how hard luck begins runnin' on a man? "

" I believe there's somethin' contagious about hard luck," said Hap Lawson. " Once a man gets the first attack of it, it's awful hard to shake off. Say, what's become of Gimpy? "

" Perhaps I can give you that information," spoke up Lou Dodge, who couldn't keep out of such a crowd as this. " The last report on Gimpy was to the effect that he, on a running horse, was hitting the high places to southward."

" He's gone? " ejaculated Hap Lawson.

" Yes, he's gone, Hap. He came to me and said this climate was disagreein' with him and he thought he'd better change."

" Well, now, ain't that too bad," Johnny Granger said sadly. " I wanted him to go down to the feed corral and curry my horse. That fool bronc, he slept in wet manure last night and he's an awful mess. I know Gimpy woulda curried him and washed him up if he had been here. Hap, you go down there and clean up my horse."

" And you go to hell and stay there! " Hap retorted. " I'm goin' yonder and see what's makin' Bill Wallace look so solemn and undecided."

He went, but he was accompanied by his two fellow-ghosts.

"Morning', Mr. Wallace," Johnny Granger began.

"Mornin', Mr. Wallace," took up Hap. "We were just wonderin'——"

"Mornin', Mr. Wallace," Tom Jones said sadly. "You look a little gaunt this mornin'. We were just awonderin' whether you've ever had any experience with ghosts."

The owner of the Double W shot them a quick, suspicious look, and then said emphatically and profanely that he had not. He whirled and stamped away, almost falling as his toe caught upon a railroad tie. He regained his balance.

"Those goddamned fool cow-waddies! Either they was in on that ghost business or they've heard about it. I sure won't tell them I was scared by a ghost—I mean ghosts. They scared forty years off the wrong end of my life, and I'd likely be runnin' yet if I hadn't stumbled over a sagebrush. Say, say, I wonder if they'd keep that ghost business under their hats if I'd give my consent for Enid to marry that damned worthless Villard boy?"

That set him to thinking of Jim Villard's father, and as a consequence he changed direction and trotted toward the railroad depot to find out what progress, if any, the senior Villard was making with Wes Moreland, the railroad agent.

Pulling at Jim's arm, Enid told him that Judge Jones was headed toward the Club Saloon.

"Jim, if he ever gets in there he'll never come out. We've just got to see him!"

"All right, honey, all right," said Jim, who just then was talking with Lou Dodge. "Let him go in and I'll pull him out with a rope."

"Well, now," chortled Lou Dodge, lifting his brows. "Who are you two going to sue?"

"We're not going to sue anybody, Lou," Enid flared,

but flushed. " I'm going to talk to the judge about putting my fool father in jail if he doesn't get some sense into his head. That's what we want to see the judge for."

" Sure it is, except you said only half of it," Jim said with quick soberness. " I want to talk to Judge Jones about seein' what procedure I've got to take to put my father in an insane asylum if he don't quit acting such a fool."

" Well, now, I can head off the judge if that's the case," offered Lou Dodge. " You two just leave it to me and I'll head him off for you."

" No, I reckon not, Lou," Jim corrected. " You see, this is a delicate, sensitive business. I'll manage to cut him out before he gets through the batwing doors. You trail along, Enid."

Bill Wallace arrived at the railroad depot as George Villard, pounding the counter with a fist and stamping the floor with one foot then the other, was telling Agent Moreland that he'd never ship another head of cattle on this railroad if he was charged even one dollar demurrage for holding the forty cattle cars for three days.

" I'm sorry, Mr. Villard," said Moreland when he could get in a word, " but that's according to railroad regulations. Each day you hold a cattle car it will cost you two dollars, and two times forty is eighty."

" I don't give a damn if it's two hundred dollars a day on each car! " Villard stormed as he thumped the counter. " I won't pay it! By drat, I won't be imposed on that way. If you've got any demurrage to assess against anybody, charge it against Bill Wallace! If it hadn't been for that old fool, my beef would have been half way to San Francisco by this time, and you know it! "

Keeping himself where he could hear and not be seen, Bill Wallace showed remarkable force of will by not rushing in and dragging Villard out. He even mentally congratulated himself on being such a patient man, adding this, however:

"I'll choke the old son-of-a-bitch to death just as soon as he gets this demurrage business settled."

"I'm sorry, Mr. Villard," Moreland said. "You'll have to pay two dollars for each of those forty cars, or I'll send them on to some other place where cattle are being shipped. Now, don't lose your temper, Mr. Villard. If it was the other way around and Bill Wallace had to wait three days to ship, I'm sure he'd pay that demurrage without raising half the fuss you're raising."

"You bet, you bet!" chortled Wallace, putting himself into view. "Wes Moreland knows I ain't a penny-pinchin' son-of-a-bitch like you are, Villard. Trouble with you is, you tried to outwit me and out-bully me and out-fight me. Come out here, and I'll wipe up the dust with you, Villainous!"

"By drat, I'll accept that challenge," Villard panted, "and after I've killed you, Wallace, I'll go back in there and tell Moreland I'll build a railroad of my own which will treat cattle owners decent when they want to ship their cattle—that is, with the exception of you."

Wallace backed up as Villard stamped out, though it was merely to give his hated enemy room. To his surprise Villard stopped when a little way outside the depot. Wallace was actually hopeful that for once he'd admit he was wrong.

"Well, what's gripin' in your craw now, Villard?" Wallace taunted.

"Now, look here, Wallace," Villard snarled as his eyes blazed and his thin lips tightened. "My patience has stood all it can endure off such a fool as you. Have you got a gun on you?"

"No, I ain't, but I can soon get one. What about a gun?"

"Then get one! Heel yourself!" Villard ordered in a purring voice. "I've got one in my valise at the Astor House yonder. While you're gettin' yours, I'll get mine."

"Now," Bill Wallace agreed and actually smiled, "George, you're talkin' sense. Let's carry this thing off without rousin' the suspicions of the sheriff.   Right yonder in the middle of the street?"

"Right there in the middle of the street," Villard said and actually smiled.

CHAPTER FIFTEEN

MEN WHO had left their work to see what became of this new trouble between Wallace and Villard, returned to their saloons and stores. Some of them cursed in disgust because there had not been a shooting scrape—at least a good, soul-inspiring fight!

The three ghosts and bandits of the previous night backed their horses away from the hitchrail in front of the Oriental Saloon, and dragged themselves into their saddles. In front of the Club Saloon, Brookins was telling his listeners how the Circle 22 beef had come to be strung out along the barbed wire fence, bawling to be let in.

"Here's the way it was, friends.   Them beef was bedded down all right, yonder beyond the shippin' pens. Then somethin' skeers 'em so they head for somewhere, which causes me to get convinced they head north because they'd been skeered from the south.   Then they slow down and start to drift west, and the more they drift west, they began to smell familiar smells, them familiar smells bein' the big stubble field of the home place of the Circle 22. So that's the way it all happened, men.   What's wrong with George Villard, anyway?"

"There's nothin' wrong with Villard," said a listener. "He's just actin' natural. Ain't he actin' natural to you, Brookins?"

"Well, yes, he is," the big straw boss from the Circle 22 home ranch said.   "Now that you remind me of it, he's the most even-tempered man I ever worked for—cantankerous as hell all the time. Now, what do you reckon sort of ants in his pants? Yonder he is marchin' fast toward the Astor House."

Between the Astor House and Club Saloon, Enid Wallace and Jim Villard were talking seriously to Justice of the Peace Jones. The short judge seemed to be listening with extreme judiciousness, keeping his long, white whiskers wagging and occasionally vehemently nodding his hoary head. He was the first of the trio to see George Villard hurrying toward the Astor House.

"Yes, after mature deliberation and sober cogitation, I advise you both to do it. Seems under the existin' circumstances to be the best thing that could be done."

Enid, starting to smile now, forgot even that much of a smile as she saw Jim's father walking stiffly and fast toward the entrance of the Astor House.

"Jim, there's your father—right back there! Turn around!"

"Oh, I don't want to see the old cuss," Jim growled. "I've got happier things to think about now. Is there anything wrong with him?"

"Yes, there is, Jim, but I don't know what it is. He isn't—he isn't acting natural."

"Then, by God," Jim cried, "is he actually in a good humour? If he is, he's not natural. Do you suppose he bulldozed the railroad company into lettin' him have those cars without demurrage? If he did, he's a smarter male parent than I thought he was."

"Beyond the slightest peradventure of a little doubt," Justice of the Peace Jones told them gravely, "get the necessary preliminaries arranged, such as competent witnesses and the like, and come over to my office in— well, say a couple of hours—and I, as presidin' Justice of the Peace in this here township will fix up the main details. Are you both sure you want to do it?"

"Oh, yes, yes, Judge!" Enid cried. "I just can't tolerate my own father any longer. Is it the same with you, Jim?"

" The same," Jim declared as his jaw muscles corded, " it's a heap more so, Enid. It may be wrong for me to say this, but I just can't put up with him any longer. See you later, Judge, and thank you a heap. By the way, how much do I owe you? "

" Now, let me see," Judge Jones said very gravely. " Do you think ten dollars will be too steep? "

" Are you ready to go back to your house, honey? "

" Yes, I think so," she said, but apparently without much enthusiasm.

She was about to take his arm in order that he could not possibly escape, when she stopped, stiffened, stared in bewilderment at her own father who was marching stiffly from the Empire Hotel toward the middle of street.

The next moment, from the tail of her right eye, she saw coming out of the Astor House, travelling with much the same speed that characterised her father, George Villard.

She grabbed Jim's arm so hard that he uttered a mild oath and told her to quit pinching.

" But, Jim, I'm not pinching! What's wrong with your father and my father? They're heading straight toward each other and look at their faces! They're going to do something terrible. Can't we stop them?"

" Oh, let 'em go," Jim Villard drawled. " They both got such a mad up, they've got to settle this sooner or later. Let 'em fight it out. They won't do each other any harm. They're just like a pair of old toothless dogs not ready to be satisfied until they decide which is the better dog. Don't worry, Enid. They been at it for years, and they're both alive."

" But if one of them should seriously hurt the other one, Jim," Enid protested.

" This is just the time for them to hurt each other good and plenty," Jim declared. " Let 'em go to it. Want to stay and watch? I do."

" Yes, yes, I think I do," she murmured, eyes wide with fear.

This fear did not diminish when Enid saw her father angle to his right, and a moment later saw Villard angle to his right as though they were going to make the axis of their battle the middle of the dusty street.

" But, Jim, Jim," she begged. " I think they have guns! "

" Oh, shucks," Jim scoffed and then laughed. " Neither of them ever carried a gun and you know it, and if they've got guns, neither of them could hit the inside of a barn if he was inside it."

Just before the determined enemies reached the middle of the street they stopped; Villard barked:

" Wallace, you cattle stealin' old reprobate, are you ready? "

" Let her go! " roared Wallace. " You money-pinchin' old cattle stealin' son-of-a-bitch! "

The next moment they were shooting at each other across the distance of about sixty feet with Smith and Wesson double-action .38 calibre pocket guns. Enid was holding her breath, expecting that each time Villard's gun exploded her father would totter and fall. Before they had fired three shots apiece, men were running from four directions, mostly out of hotels and saloons.

" Somebody help! Somebody help! " Enid shrilled when she could find her voice. " Don't let them kill each other! Please don't let them kill each other! They're just a couple of old fools! "

Jim Villard, advancing with swift, long strides into the street, seemed to be doing it with serene deliberation. Just as his father's Smith and Wesson exploded for the fifth time, Jim lunged upon him, wrenched away the gun and poked it into hip pocket. He grasped his father by his dirty shirt collar.

" Now, Dad, that'll be enough of this damned foolishness," he snarled. " I'm plumb tired of it."

For about half a minute the senior Villard tried to

wrench free, but seeing he could not accomplish this, he began to threaten and argue. He'd be eternally damned if he'd be bossed and disciplined by any son of his! He didn't even have honour and manhood about him to choose a decent girl to keep company with.

"Shut up, Dad," Jim growled, "or I'll ram those words down your stubborn throat! Don't say another word about her."

"Go ahead and shove them down his throat, Jim," ordered Enid, who was close by now. "There isn't a word of truth in what he says and he knows it."

"I'll kill the dirty-minded old bastard!" argued Bill Wallace, wondering why he hadn't brought along at least five extra cartridges for his revolver.

Then he was pounced upon from behind, and thrown to the ground, face first.

"That'll be more'n plenty of this, Wallace," Sheriff Smith ordered. "I'm plumb tired and disgusted with these old fools, Jim. I want him too. We're going to my jail!"

"Enid, don't you let this fool Smith disgrace me by puttin' me in his calaboose!" ordered Wallace. "Don't you do it!"

"Oh, I was going to put you there, anyway, Dad," Enid said in a shaking voice. "But I was going to have you arrested only for being crazy. Now you've tried to kill another man. I'm sorry, but I don't think I can do anything for you."

"No, Enid, you can't," the sheriff agreed. "This time they've gone and done it—assaultin' each other with deadly weapons with intent to kill. They won't get out, if I can keep them in, you can bet your last chip on that."

"Huh, what's that? What's that?" exploded Villard, just beginning to realise what was about to be done. "By the eternal gods, the man never lived who could put me in jail. Have you forgotten who I am? I'm a rich, respectable cattleman!"

K

" You may be rich enough and have cows enough," said Johnny Granger, " but it looks to me, Villard, anybody who said you were respectable would sure be stretchin' the truth."

At that moment Dobie Dick Donovan and Brazos Cobb arrived, and in no good humour as the shooting had interrupted their friendly poker game.

" Do you think two old stags like this are tryin' to steal our gun slingin', Dobie? " inquired Brazos Cobb.

" It looks like it, and that's our right. We should kill 'em both."

" Just reach for a gun, and I'll kill you both," growled the sheriff.

Now Villard began to protest vehemently against being taken to jail. He was a rich and respectable cattleman, wasn't he? Never before in his life had he fired a shot at a fellow man.

" Well, by God," Bill Wallace promised, " the next time there's shootin', I'm goin' to use a scattergun and I'm goin' to hit you! I borrowed that damned peashooter off Hitchcock. He said it'd kill a man and I made the mistake of believin' him. Leggo my ear, Andy Smith. By God, you'll get into trouble! "

" And you'll get into trouble, Bill, if you don't march along with me like a good boy," the sheriff corrected. " Jim, push your father over here so I can get ahold of one of his ears. I ain't got my handcuffs, but they'll come along when I get a hold of one of their ears."

" Dratted if I will, Smith! " Villard stormed. " I don't suffer any such shame and humiliation as being led around by my ears."

" All right," said the sheriff, " if you don't want me to lead you by the ear, I'll put a twitch on your nose, then you'll sure come along. Hey, somebody, get me a little piece of stout board and bore a quick hole in the end of it and get me a piece of strong cord. Somebody certainly knows how to make a twitch."

" Hey, all of us knows what a twitch is, or if they don't

they're durn fools," somebody shouted. "Say, lend me a piece of pine. I got a good whittlin' knife. Anybody got a stray hoggin' string about him?"

"I sure have!" yipped Johnny Granger. "I got a couple of 'em here on my person somewhere. Here they are. I'm usin' 'em for a belt."

"But, Johnny, Johnny," protested Tom Jones in simulated horror, "you'll lose your pants if you take off your belt. They're my spare pants and they're way too big for you."

"I know, Tom," Johnny agreed placidly as he removed one hogging string and left the other for a belt. "Plumb overlooked tellin' you that when I borrowed these here pants from you one of them pockets contained fifty-five cents."

"Then hand it back, Granger," Tom snorted. "I been rackin' my brain to death wonderin' what become of that fifty-five cents.

Now the sheriff showed how two men could be led to his jail, each by an ear. After about forty yards of this, Villard balked, sitting back like a stubborn mule, declaring that he had business to attend to.

"What business, Dad?" demanded Jim Villard, who, with Enid, was in the vanguard of the following procession. "If it's not too important business I'll take care of it for you."

"You'll take care of no business for me!" Villard yelled. "By drat, no! Where's Brookins? Brookins, come here!"

The tall straw boss of the Circle 22 came and stood but without the bowed head of humility.

"What you want, Villard? When you want them cattle shipped? I'll tend to it, but I'd rather not."

"I don't want you to ship my cattle," Villard growled. "Dobie Dick Donovan will tend to gettin' them into the cars and shippin' 'em. You go over to that depot and tell Moreland that regardless of what he says the railroad rules are I won't pay him a dratted red cent in demurrage for holdin' them forty empty cattle cars! Add my compliments, too."

" Thanks for your compliments, Mr. Villard," drawled the railroad agent, who was in the crowd. " But when it comes to you gettin' out of demurrage, there ain't any more chance of that than there is of you goin' to heaven. According to railroad regulations it's costin' you eighty dollars a day to hold those forty empty cattle cars. You're already owin' the railroad a small part of the second eighty dollars."

" I'll ship my beef in those cars and I won't pay any demurrage! Eighty dollars a day, why, it's an outrage, gentlemen! I wouldn't be a bit surprised, providin' I pay that sum, that Moreland there puts about two-thirds of it into his own pocket. What are you lingerin' here for, Sheriff? Wastin' my good time! I want to get to your damned jail as soon as I can so I can send for my lawyer! "

" Which won't do you much good, Villard, or you, Wallace," the sheriff growled as he got them moving again. " I'm going to charge each of you with assault with a deadly weapon with intent to kill, and that's an offence you can't easily get bail on. Don't argue with me because both of you put together couldn't persuade me to make it disturbing the peace and quiet of Big Sage."

An hour later, Jim Villard and Enid Wallace sat alone and not very close together on the edge of the Edwards' porch. Jim looked as though he'd been drawn through a knot hole several sizes too small because of what he'd seen and heard.

" Jim, I feel like an old woman," murmured Enid, who looked utterly exhausted.

" Now, you look here, honey," Jim vetoed, " you sure don't look like an old woman to me. You still look just like my sweetheart. Ain't you? "

" Yes, I am," she said with a courageous smile and a little more spirit. " But, Jim, what we went through is most exhaustin'. You think we should still go on through with our plans."

"Sure, we'll go through with them," he said with plenty of spirit now. "Don't you think we should, honey?"

"Yes, I think we should, Jim," she murmured and closed her tired eyes.

CHAPTER SIXTEEN

GEORGE VILLARD had bluffed and bulldozed for so long and so successfully that he did not actually believe he was going to be jailed until he was led into the county bastille by an ear, which was being pinched thoroughly by an angry sheriff, who had Mr. Villard's left ear between forefinger and thumb.

Seeing that he was going to be incarcerated, Villard exploded with righteous indignation. He threatened, cajoled, beseeched, even offered the sheriff a hundred dollars if he were allowed to go free.

"How much will you pay me, Bill?" Andy Smith inquired.

"Not a damned cent! I'm goin' to have a fine time bein' in jail with that varmint. Put us in adjoinin' cells as I want good company."

"Oh, my God, my God," Villard said and groaned. "Put me anywhere, Smith, but in a cell next to him. I may lose my sanity and choke him to death between the bars."

"That's just what I'm hopin' you two will do," the sheriff advised. "Here you go. These are my two best cells. They are supposed to be clean."

Wallace entered as if happy when told to go into his cell. Its lock clicked.

"Now, he's where he can't cause any more trouble, Andy," Villard begged. "Set me free and I'll make it worth your while. As you know I've got a lot of political influence in this county."

" The political influence you've got anywhere," Wallace taunted, spitting tobacco juice on the bare floor, " could be put where your brains are, Villard, which occupies a space about as big as one end of a peanut shell. Don't let him talk you out of it, Andy."

" Don't lose any sleep about that, Wallace," the sheriff growled. " I've got half of you two where I want you, and now I'm goin' to get the other half. Villard, if your not going in there under your own steam, I'm going to kick you in! Get in! "

Villard stamped with what he thought majesty into the small cell. Its lock clicked.

" Now you two fraternise," the sheriff ordered. " Be sociable together now, like your wagon bosses are around town. I'm just comin' to believe how Dobie Dick and Brazos are the only sensible men around Big Sage."

" A pair of ignorant, unprincipled fools," Villard corrected with a haughty snort. " Sheriff, do me the favour of telling Donovan to call upon me here. I have orders to give him."

" While you're at it, Andy," Wallace said, " tell Brazos to make me a sociable visit here in my new home. I want to tell him to round up my gang and take 'em back to the ranch. They're through work here."

" What about those forty steers you got mixed with my cattle? " Villard snorted. " Who's goin' to part them out and take care of 'em? By the eternal, I won't let my riders do it! "

" Why, I thought, George, that you'd ship my forty steers with your beef," Wallace said as a hurt look rushed to his weathered face. " Won't you accommodate me by doin' that? "

" Accommodate you! Wallace, here's how I'd like to accommodate you—by makin' sure you got a swift trip to hell! "

" Now, what do you think of such a remark as that,

Andy?" Wallace said, staring with mock incredulity at Smith. "And that from the most righteous man in Nevada. Ain't you plumb amazed like I am?"

The sheriff managed to keep back a grin. "What do you want now, Villard?"

Almost snapping his words apart, the owner of the Circle 22 asked the sheriff to send Mr. Jefferson Dinwoodie to him as soon as possible.

"Now I know he's no sport," uttered Wallace. "He's got to have a lawyer to try to screw him out of jail. Why, damn it, Villainous, you know it's just where you've belonged for the last thirty years."

Acknowledging this with no more than a contemptuous snort, Villard said, "If you see my son Jim, Sheriff, tell him I need him here at the earliest possible moment."

The sheriff's progress to Main Street was slow because of the many questions he had to answer. He answered them all very much in the same words like this:

"They're just fine—gettin' along like a couple of long separated brothers."

The comments to his answer were very much the same, like this: "Yeah, like a pair of old tomcats thrown over a clothes-line with their tails tied together."

Big Sage at this time had two attorneys-at-law. One was Jefferson Dinwoodie, a short, pompous, paunchy man, with a florid face, a big red nose, and sagging jowls. His too tight trousers and cutaway coat were the garments he had worn when he had arrived in Big Sage eleven years earlier.

Jefferson Dinwoodie had an office of sorts, but when not there, he could usually be found with his polished left boot on a bar rail and an empty glass in his right hand. So did the sheriff find him in the Silver Star Saloon. His eyes brightened with hope as the sheriff ambled in, seeing the prospect of a free drink. Instead of suggesting this, the sheriff said:

"Jeff, Villainous Villard wants to see you. He's in my jail."

" So I've heard! So I've heard! " the lawyer said thickly. " At first I failed to let my ears believe that such an outrage could have happened in this fair city, but now that I have it from a fairly reliable source, I can no further doubt the truth of that rumour. What does Mr. Villard want me for? "

" Because you're not a beauty, Jeff, it's my hunch he wants to consult you on some matter of law," said the sheriff.

" By the way, Sheriff, when you incarcerated Villard, did you go through his pockets? No offence meant, Mr. Sheriff, but an experienced peace officer would naturally search the person of a man he locks in a cell. Speaking of money, how much did you find on him? "

" Damn it, I don't know, Jeff, I didn't search him for money, I just took his pocket-knife away from him, as I'd already disarmed him of that pea-shootin' pistol he tried to kill Wallace with."

" Now, let me thoroughly understand you, Andy," the lawyer said. " Did Mr. George Villard actually make an attempt to take the life of Mr. William Wallace? "

" Well, I don't know whether he was trying to take Bill's life or not but I do happen to know he was shootin' fast at him with the intent to kill."

" And what you've just said, Sheriff, causes me to believe without peradventure of a doubt," said the lawyer, " that you have charged Mr. Villard with a felony."

The sheriff said with a jerky nod and one word that that was correct.

Moving cautiously away from the bar, Mr. Dinwoodie got himself balanced and marched grandly out with much dignity.

" How about one on the house, Sheriff? " volunteered the bartender.

" One on the house would sure suit me after what I've just gone through," said the sheriff, putting one boot on the rail. " Does anybody in here know where I can find Brazos Cobb? Bill Wallace wants him."

" Sure, I can tell you where to find Brazos," a drunk

cowboy enthused. "Him and Dobie Dick Donovan are down at the Oriental playin' two-bit poker and gettin' along fine. Why, Sheriff, I know you won't believe me, but I'm goin' to tell you the honest truth. They're actin' just like Brazos, he was an old mare, and Dobie Dick, he was her dutiful and overgrown colt, they're that happy and affectionate."

"But it won't last," the bartender remarked.

The sheriff made no comment to this, but marched out determined to finish his errands as quickly as possible so he could go before Justice of the Peace Jones and swear to felony complaints against Villard and Wallace. He was determined to keep those two in jail, at least until Big Sage could settle back to its normal tranquillity.

Having delivered his message to Brazos, the sheriff told Donovan that he was also wanted by his employer.

"Oh, I got no business with him," Dobie good-naturedly refused. "I'll see him next time, Sheriff. Tell him I'll be right here in town any time he wants them beef driven back from the home ranch and shipped. While he's decidin' on that I'm goin' to enjoy myself in the fine company of Mr. Brazos Cobb."

"And after them beef is shipped?" queried Brazos, his wrinkled lips narrowing to a mere slit. "Are we goin' to have one hell of a fine celebration, Dobie?"

"Texas man, we sure are goin' have all of that," Donovan reassured, his face for a second or two becoming a mask of bleakness. "Sure, and we're goin' to make this here town sit up on its hind legs and wag its tail!"

The sheriff started to depart, but stopped. He asked whether anybody could tell him where he could find Jim Villard.

Tom Fisk, the saddler, who couldn't work leather without whisky, said that he knew Jim Villard's whereabouts. He was at the home of Blacksmith Edwards, where he seemed to have taken up his abode.

The sheriff was stepping from the boardwalk in front of the Silver Star Saloon when he saw Judge Jones approaching from the direction of the Edwards' home. He would send the judge back to deliver the message to Jim Villard.

When they met, not far from the sheriff's office and the jail in the small brick courthouse, the sheriff told the judge what he wanted him to do, and as he did this, he had the suspicion that the old Justice of the Peace was filled with suppressed happiness and excitement.

" Turn back and tell Jim his villainous old father wants him at the jail," the sheriff ordered. " Judge, you're not near as busy as I am. Grant me that favour and I'll treat you next time we meet in a saloon."

" It won't do you no good to deliver a message to 'em now, Andy," Jones said, waggling his beard gravely. " The young feller's too busy."

" Too busy at what? Makin' love to that Wallace girl? "

" No, not that, Andy," the judge said as though correcting a dear friend. " Mrs. Edwards had got him at work."

" At work at what? Damned if I'd work for anybody if I had the opportunity to make love to Enid Wallace. What's she got him doin'? "

" Peelin' spuds," the judge said gravely. " What do you make of that, Andy? Is it a good omen or a bad omen? "

" It's sure a mighty bad sign," the sheriff said without hesitation. " When it gets to that stage there's no tellin' what's goin' to happen. Damn it, I wish this town would quiet down. There's a boy. I'll pay him a quarter and send him to deliver that message to Jim Villard. Do you think that'll stop him from peelin' Mrs. Edwards' potatoes? "

" Now, I don't know about that," Jones said soberly, but had to snicker. " If I was peelin' such potatoes such as he's peelin', I don't know whether I'd stop short of a dollar."

The troubled sheriff was trying to figure that out when

the venerable Justice of the Peace announced that he was idle for an hour or two.

" Idle, hell," the sheriff said with a snort. " Jones, I never see you doing anything, except takin' a drink if somebody'll buy it for you."

Jingling what faintly sounded like two gold coins in his right front pants pocket, the judge indignantly said that was a canard, a falsehood and a damned lie. Already to-day he'd done enough legal work for three average justices of the peace.

" I've been informed by reliable sources that you intend to file felony complaints against Villard and Wallace. Was I correctly so informed? "

" Yes," the sheriff said impatiently. " Let's go and do it now while you're in the notion. I'm goin' to keep those two old fools in my jail till they get some sense into their heads if it takes the rest of their natural lives."

" That there, Andy, meets with my wholehearted legal approval," Judge Jones said. " Tell you what we'll do, Andy, after we get through with them there complaints. We'll go over to the saloon and have a few drinks."

At this time, Lawyer Dinwoodie, keeping himself in balance by pressing his paunch against the bars of the cell, was telling George Villard that he would not accept any legal work unless he saw the colour of a respectable retainer fee.

" Well, drat it, what is a respectable legal fee for your services? " Villard demanded indignantly. " It so happens that I know, Dinwoodie, that you're willin' to pick up a dollar now and then. I'll pay you ten dollars if you'll attend to this business for me."

Forthwith, Lawyer Dinwoodie asked the nature of the business the owner of the Circle 22 wanted attended to legally.

Being, as he thought, a little shrewder than the lawyer, Villard said the nature of the business was convincing the railroad company that it could not collect demurrage on empty cattle cars that were being held and not used. He added that he did not propose under any circumstances to be robbed by any tarnation, dratted, railroad company.

" That, Mr. Villard," Dinwoodie said thickly but very impressively, " is a very serious matter frought with many potential complications. As doubtless you fail to know a railroad company is a powerful corporation with many and varied corporate ramifications, employing large and learned legal council. Mr. Villard, I regret to say that I cannot act as your local attorney for less than two hundred and fifty dollars, with fifty dollars paid now as a re-taining fee for my learned and resourceful legal services. Of course, if it were a small matter, I would be happy to attend to it for you gratis in token of our long and mutual friendliness."

" Hell, Jefferson," said Bill Wallace from the adjoining cell, " don't be a poor sport—raise him a couple of hundred and show him the railroad company and winnin' the case is a big job. Tap him five hundred."

" Damn it, Wallace," Villard exploded wrathfully, " keep your gab out of this. If you can't find anything else to do, take off your boots and play with your toes."

" I've got one boot off," chuckled Wallace who was sitting on his squeaky cot. " I'm just gettin' ready to whittle my toenails. For a big case like this, you'll be gettin' Jefferson Dinwoodie cheap at five hundred."

Villard declared that he would not pay a retaining fee of more than ten dollars, and that would be the whole fee because all he would expect of Lawyer Dinwoodie was the convincing of Agent Moreland that said George Villard was entitled to those forty empty cattle cars without demurrage for three more days.

" I'll pay that dratted, tarnation company not one red cent in demurrage! You understand what I'm tellin' you, don't you, Dinwoodie? "

"Yes, sir, I most certainly do, Mr. Villard," the paunchy lawyer said thickly. " Mr. Villard, I see clearly that I cannot represent you in this matter for a cent under fifty dollars. Ah—hem, there is my colleague and rival, Mr. Manuel Johnson. Perhaps that damned scallywag will take your case for ten dollars. I bid you a cordial good day, Villard."

" Oh, damn, pay him the fifty and don't be a cheap sport, Villard," Bill Wallace ordered. " Go ahead, Villainous, be a real sport."

" Oh, all right! " Villard said in rage and desperation. " It's just another example of my being robbed and cheated by everybody I do business with. I'll tell you what I'll do, Dinwoodie. I'm a liberal man. I'll pay you twenty-five dollars for attending to this legal business for me."

" Fifty or it's no play," Lawyer Dinwoodie said stubbornly. He turned hopefully toward Bill Wallace, who was cussing silently because the sheriff had robbed him of his pocket-knife. " Ah, Mr. Wallace, do you happen to be represented by a capable attorney, who is competent to avail himself of all legal technicalities, and if necessity dictates, employ his own brand of skull-duggery? If you've not, I'd be happy to represent you in this small trouble which involved you with the law, for the small sum of fifty dollars. Ah—hem, am I correct in the assumption that from this moment on I am your retained attorney-at-law, Mr. Wallace? "

" No, tarnation drat it, you're not his lawyer, Din-woodie! " Villard snapped, secretly groaning as though his heart were being cut into four pieces. " Wait'll I find my purse, and I'll suffer myself to be robbed of at least forty dollars."

" And I assure you, Mr. Villard, that you're making no mistake in retaining a capable attorney-at-law," Dinwoodie said thickly and impressively, as he took two double eagles and a ten. " I shall attend to this matter most thoroughly for you, Mr. Villard. Of that you may rest assured. Be of good cheer, sir."

" Ah, ah," Bill Wallace sighed. " Jefferson, at last we

have seen the performance of a miracle by Villainous Villard provin' he's a dead game sport. You know what, Villainous? "

" Yes, what? " Villard snapped. " What foolish thing have you got to say next, Wallace, you crooked old cattle thief? "

" I'll let that epithet pass for the present because of the pleasant future you and me are goin' to enjoy, George," Wallace said with what seemed to be warmth and friendship. " It won't be long before you and me'll be gettin' plenty bored by these jail cells, and to make the time pass swiftly we'll be playin' draw poker between the bars of our cells. Don't you think that's a fact, George? "

" Fact, fact! Here's what I do think, Wallace, it's just another crazy imaginin's of your crazy mind. You know well enough that I'm not a gamblin' man."

" Well, now, so you ain't, George," Bill Wallace agreed as though he were extremely sorry for Mr. Villard. " I should have noticed that when I saw Dinwoodie bluff you out of forty dollars. Jeff, send us in a checker board and some checkers—checkers is about George's size."

CHAPTER SEVENTEEN

WALLACE'S PRESENT state of mind induced by his belief that he would be extremely happy at watching Villard squirm inside a prison cell, soon vanished. He sat upon his hard cot brooding, a dark scowl upon his weathered face. He wondered how he was going to manipulate things to kill George Villard, suddenly his most hated enemy.

He could not bring the owner of the Circle 22 within reach of his big hands by taunting and threatening him and calling him names. He knew from long experience that at heart Villard was a craven coward. He would have to fetch him over to the bars by cunning. A checker game would be just the proper business. They would play checkers for a while and then he would grab the old thief, pull him against the bars and choke him to death.

"Now, I'll be right nice to him for the time bein'," Bill Wallace told himself. "I'll show him how the best way for us to pass the time here in these damned cells is for us to act like friends."

He spoke aloud, then, asking Villard how he felt.

"Very well. Very well, indeed," Villard grunted. He now lay upon his cot, staring at the fly-specked ceiling. "Don't worry about the state of my health, Wallace."

"Oh, don't be a damned fool, George," Wallace advised amiably. "There's no tellin' how long we'll have to stay in here as that fool sheriff's filed felony complaints against both of us. What you say we bury all of the hatchets but the end of the handles?"

"Drat it, no!" Villard retorted, without looking at his enemy. "I make no peace with you, Wallace, as long as you insist on that no-account daughter of yours receiving the attentions of my son."

"Then make your damned worthless son keep away from her!" Wallace shouted. "She's a girl, and as a consequence she ain't got no sense, except she believes she wants to get married to something like that boy of yours. Maybe he's got sense enough to understand what you tell him."

"I'm afraid he hasn't," Villard muttered and groaned.

Bill Wallace might have taunted him into a fight, then, but for the noise of somebody coming into the end of the short, gloomy jail corridor. It proved to be Brazos Cobb, his big spur rowels rolling on the floor, his holstered forty-five against his scrawny thigh.

"Howday, Bill," said Brazos in his slow, southern drawl. "You look just fine in there. Never knew before how contented you look in a jail cell."

"Shut your damned mouth, Brazos," ordered his employer.

"Yes, be silent," ordered Villard. "If you've got nothing better than that to say, take yourself away. I have some sober thinking to do. Why didn't that wagon boss of mine come with you?"

"Oh, you mean Dobie Dick, don't you, Mr. Villard? He says he's takin' a fine, big vacation and he don't want to be bothered with you. He says he'll be right on hand, though, when you make up your mind when you want to ship them beef of yours. Made up your mind to pay them demurrage charges to the railroad, and round up your beef from the home ranch and ship 'em?"

"That," snapped Villard, as he hid his eyes with the flat of a hand, "is my own personal business and I'll attend to it at the proper time."

"Well, the proper time for me not to talk to you, Mr. Villard," accepted Brazos, "is right now."

Brazos moved to where he could look directly into the other cell. As he did this, Wallace rose, came quickly toward the barred door, signalling Indian talk fashion, until he was near enough to whisper:

"Give me that gun, Brazos, and let me shoot that old son-of-a-bitch! I'll hand the gun right back to you."

"Yes, I guess not," Brazos said, moving backwards. "Doin' it that way would make it look like I did it—with me holdin' a smokin' gun in my hand. Oh, no, Bill! You'll have to get up earlier than that. Want to try again?"

Wallace demanded to be told whether Brazos were going to take the ranch crew and head for home.

"Yeah, I got the crew on their way now," Brazos said.

"And you'll be ridin', say in the mornin', Brazos?"

"No, I ain't agoin' to ride out in the mornin'," Brazos said softly, yet with a hard determination. "I'll be goin' when I get good and ready. Me and Dobie Dick, we're goin' to wind it all up in a big celebration. Just came to report that I'd sent out the rest of the riders—sent 'em hightailin' it, too, because they savvy who's wagon boss of the Double W."

"Well, I'm the big boss of the Double W, because I happen to own it," Wallace growled as he shook the bars. "Brazos, I want you to light out for the ranch not later than to-morrow morning."

"Boss, I think you better make another guess at that," Brazos advised. "Me and Dobie Dick have got quite a bit of fun ahead of us and quite a bit of work before we come to that big celebration of ours."

"Ride down to the river place of the Circle 22 and part out them forty steers of mine that old cuss caused to be mixed with his. Drive 'em up here and put 'em in the pen and ship 'em. They'll fill two cars. Tell Moreland about it."

"No, you don't!" cried out Villard, as he sprang to his feet. "You don't put any schemin' like that over on me. Them forty Double W steers stay in my field and eat my stubble and hay till I get ready to let 'em out! When I get ready to ship, I'll bring 'em up here with my cattle."

"Yes, by God," Wallace stormed, "and ship 'em as your beef and I won't get a cent out of 'em!"

As though Wallace's rage had blown him back, Villard sank to his cot and carried with him a very cheerful thought. For every Double W steer eating Villard hay and stubble, he would charge Wallace two dollars. George Villard, owner of the great Circle 22, wanted to slap his leg and sing with glee. Were not two times forty eighty dollars—the exact sum the dratted railroad was charging him per day for demurrage on those forty unused cars? The next moment, he looked as if stricken with a fit of pain.

"Why, what's the matter, George?" Wallace demanded in actual concern. "Have you got a gripe? Has one of your guts got twisted round all your others?"

"By God," exclaimed Brazos. "I do believe the man's sick. Had I best go for a doctor, Bill?"

"No," corrected Wallace as he remembered that he

and Villard were enemies. " Let the old varmint die.
It'll save me the trouble of killin' him."

" All right, boss," Brazos accepted good-naturedly.
" I'll ride down right away and part out them forty
Double W beef and drive 'em up here and ship 'em as
you say. I'll get Dobie Dick to help me."

" By drat, no hired man of mine helps the Double W! "
Villard warned, getting to his feet, his mental agony
changing to rage. " Tell Donovan to stay right here in
town till I tell him what's to be done. Those forty
Double W beef stay right in my field till I say what's to
be done with them."

" Until I say what's to be done with them," Wallace
swore. " And I'm sayin' right now, and you heard me,
they're comin' out."

" You bet your last white chip on that, Bill," drawled
Brazos. " They're comin' out right soon because I
say so, and my fine friend Dobie Dick is goin' to say so
too."

This time Brazos left, and in a hurry, taking with him
an extremely bright and stimulating idea. He had to
find Dobie Dick immediately and tell him about it.
Brazos wanted to swear with glee, but he'd barely stepped
from the sheriff's office when he slid to a stop.

There, coming in, was the handsomest, unembarrassed
young couple he had ever seen. Brazos actually blushed
with embarrassment when he recognised them. Then he
ejaculated:

" Hell, where you two going? "

" Why, Jim's going in to see his father," Enid said a
little breathlessly. " A boy came down a little while ago
and told him his father wanted to see him in the jail."

" Well, he's not much to look at in the jail," Brazos
said, not knowing what else to say. " My God, Jim,
where'd you get them there store clothes? They sure
fit you just beautiful. You didn't look too good to me
before, but now I got to admit, you're kind of handsome.
Enid, I'll be damned if I blame you much for wantin'

to marry up with him. I hope he's not half as mean as his father."

"He isn't!" she said and then crimsoned to the roots of her dark hair. "There isn't a mean thing about Jim."

"Well, I wouldn't go that far," said Brazos.

"Jim, honey, don't pay any attention to Brazos," Enid whispered. "He always talks this way. He doesn't mean anything though,"

"Go on in, you two," said Brazos. "I got some important business to attend to with Dobie Dick Donovan."

"Do you know what my father wants me for, Brazos?" Jim inquired.

"No, I don't, Jimmy," Brazos said as if extremely sad. "Your old man, Jimmy, he never confides anything confidential to me, me bein' a Double W man. Adios."

CHAPTER EIGHTEEN

THOUGH ENID, like about everybody else in the Big Sage country, had heard much of George Villard's disposition, she had no more than a speaking acquaintance with him. As they entered the sheriff's office, she told herself that Daniel, when he had entered the lion's den, must have felt much as she did.

She had not really wanted to come, but Jim had persuaded her by explaining that she would eventually have to get acquainted with his father. He had added:

"You won't find him agreeable, Enid. He isn't that way even to his friends."

"But can a man like he is have friends?" she asked.

"Now that you mention it, honey, I doubt that he really has a single friend. Of course, I would stand up for him if I saw his life was in danger."

They went on into the gloomy shadow of the jail corridor. The two rich prisoners heard them coming, but in the gloom could not identify them except as one person. Not until the barred sunlight coming in through a window struck them did Bill Wallace and George Villard identify them. The ranchers stiffened, their mouths dropped open, snapped shut. Bill Wallace's fierce eyes were not upon the well-dressed young man, but upon his cool daughter. He rose slowly from where he sat on the cot, stalked to the bars and gripped two of them.

"Hallo, Dad," Enid said a little breathlessly.

"Don't talk to me!" he exploded, "except to tell me what are you doin' runnin' around with that worthless whelp? Didn't I tell you to keep away from him? Ain't you got any pride, or respect for me?"

Before she could say anything to that if she'd been able to speak, Villard, who was up gripping two bars, released them and turned upon Wallace.

"Pride! Pride!" he roared. "What are you talkin' about, Wallace? Do you think she's sufferin' loss of pride by associatin' with my son? By drat, if you want my honest opinion of that, I think it's him that's sufferin' by associatin' with her!"

"Oh, for God's sake," Jim cried out. "Father, stop bein' a fool. There's no pride involved here, and if there is, it strikes me that you might look around and find some. You wanted to see me?"

"Yes, I did!" roared Villard. "But I didn't want to see you in the company of that wench! I want to tell you what to do about those beef that in some manner got down to the home ranch. But I'll get somebody else to tend to that."

"That'll suit me fine!" Jim said with forced calm. "As things have turned out, I've got plenty to do here in town."

"Wench!" Wallace exploded, as he grasped two of the partition bars. "Why, you damned old hypocrite, Villard, if what I've heard is true, you lived with squaws when you were young! Don't you allude to my daughter as a wench! By God, if you do, I'll rip out two of these bars and beat you to death with them. Come over here and let me get a hold of you, and I'll choke you to death —no, I'll pull you between two of these bars and that'll finish you!"

As Wallace threatened to do this, he was actually so fierce, so brutal looking, that Enid clutched Jim's arm, and Jim's father recoiled until the underside of his knees caught on the edge of the cot and he sat down with a thump, bumping the back of his head against the wall.

"There," Wallace chuckled. "Go ahead and do that a few more times and beat your own self to death—callin' my girl a wench. If I didn't think your boy was just a little better than you are, I'd call him a drunken buck Indian! Enid, what do you mean by runnin' around with him, anyway?"

Though she was as pale as a sun-tanned ghost could ever be, there was fire, not tears, in her brown eyes, and her pretty chin was up. She could feel Jim tremble.

"Mr. Wallace," Jim said, forcing himself to calmness. "Don't you think you'd best know what you're talkin' about, before you talk any more on that subject? I love Enid and I'm not ashamed of it, and I'm sure that she loves me."

"Of course I love you, Jim!" Enid cried out, squeezing his arm to prove it. "Dad, I came along with him to see if we couldn't make you get some sense."

"Sense! Sense!" growled her father, pointing angrily at the man in the next cell. "What about him gettin' some sense in his head? He's responsible for all this trouble! If it hadn't been for him there wouldn't have been any trouble!"

"That," said the senior Villard, with high self-righteousness, "is a dratted lie, Wallace. I never opposed my son associatin' with your daughter till I found out they was keepin' company."

"I ain't talkin' about them," Wallace cursed. "I'm talkin' about the way you mixed up them herds outside the shippin' pens. If you had held your herd back like a decent man should have done, everything would have gone off fine."

"And," said Villard, "let you have first chance at them forty cattle cars you stole from me? Tarnation drat! I should have had the law on you for that!"

"Yes, the law of your stubborn will," Wallace taunted. "That's the trouble with you, Villard. You always thought you were the law yourself over here in this range country, and, by God, you ain't! I had forty empties ordered and them was my forty empties on the shippin' pen spur, and you know it! You just wanted to crawl in and steal 'em for your cattle. It'd serve you right if you had to pay five hundred dollars a day demurrage on them other forty empties, which is on the spur now."

"Jim, hadn't we better be going?" Enid whispered, wondering how much longer she could keep back a rush of angry, shamed tears.

"Yes, we'll be goin' now," Jim said, laying an arm about her shoulders. "There isn't anything to be gained by staying here and trying to talk to these old fools. Come on, honey girl."

"All right, sweetheart," she said loudly and defiantly. "You and I understand each other, Jim, don't we? We never quarrel, but I don't understand why you're so very different from your father."

"Enid, honey, and I don't understand how you're so different from your father," Jim said as he tightened his arm about her shoulders and drew her closer. "I reckon you must take after your mother."

That demonstration of affection was just a little too much for the imprisoned ranchers. They reacted instantly. They stood stiff, pale, staring at the retreating couple, which even in their rage, they secretly admitted made a handsome pair.

"Now, by drat," cried out Villard, who was first to find his voice, "she's got him completely under her spell.

I've just got to swear! By God, that girl of yours is a designin' witch, Wallace!"

"And that son of yours, Villard," cried Wallace, " is a damned dirty, schemin' skunk, makin' my daughter fall in love with him like she has done. I'm sorry to have to admit it, but ever since she's been a little girl, Villard, Enid hasn't had full sense."

"Then, by drat, that's all the more reason I don't propose to have her marryin' my son!"

"Now wait, and let me finish, you old interferin' buzzard!" Wallace ordered, shaking two bars. "Here's the main reason I don't want 'em to get married—they're both half-wits, and bein' half-wits, what'll their children be but a pack of idiots? Here's how I figure it, Villard, you old polecat, multiply a half-wit by a half-wit and what do you get—a quarter-wit. You've got little enough sense, no wonder the boy hasn't much sense!"

Spent by rage and frustration, especially by being cooped up in two jail cells, Villard and Wallace flopped limply to their cots, and sat there, chins in hands, staring, not at each other, but at the dirty floor. They felt strange indeed, being out of venom like a couple of aged rattlesnakes that had broken off their last set of fangs.

Outside, Enid was ready to burst into tears, and Jim into violent cursing when they saw Jefferson Dinwoodie coming at a dignified waddling walk, which, with the lawyers's utmost effort, was keeping in a more or less straight line.

"By gosh, Jeff Dinwoodie is really drunk this time, ain't he, Enid?" Jim demanded and had to grin. "Say, honey, if I ever get as much belly as Jeff's got, get an axe and hew it off, won't you? Isn't he a specimen?"

"And if you ever get as much paunch as he's got," Enid said and had to laugh, " I'll kill you—honest I will, Jim. He's a shame and a disgrace, wastin' his education and learning. Dad says he's an exceptional lawyer."

"Don't tell me what your dad says," Jim growled. "I just heard enough from him."

" Well, he's as good as your father is," she said.

They would have probably quarrelled then and there had not Mr. Jefferson Dinwoodie come to a teetering stop in front of them. It was evident immediately that in their unusual clothes he did not recognise them. He cleared his throat, sucked back some slobber, and then as he bowed gallantly, his heavy paunch and his heavy shoulders almost toppled him over on to his head. He regained his balance with several grunts and a few jerks, and after he got back on his feet, he apologised thickly and profusely for his unusual physical conduct by explaining that he had rheumatism in his right knee and his left hip.

By this time, instead of being ready to quarrel with Jim, Enid was ready to giggle. In a sober drawl, Jim said that he was very sorry to learn that Mr. Dinwoodie was so afflicted. He surveyed Jim and his bleary eyes slyly blinked his fat lids. He cleared his throat, and with expression of apology, said:

" Er—ahem, young man, I'm sorry to confess that you have the advantage of me, as does this most beautiful young lady. Will you—will you think that I am presumptious if I be candid enough to inform you that you are, beyond peradventure of a doubt, the handsomest pair of newly-weds I've seen in many a moon? Will you be—be, in many moons, generous enough to accept the many moons, sincere congratulations of Mr. Jefferson Din—Dinwoodie, attorney-at-law? You names, many moons, if you care to so honour a highly respectable— many a moon, to the bar."

" To the bar is right," Enid exploded in an outburst of laughter when she could find her voice. " Jim, I'm going. I've just got to go."

" Well, I'm going too," agreed Jim, with forced soberness. " Glad to make your acquaintance, Mr. Dinwoodie, but it so happens just now we don't need a lawyer."

" Well, by God, many moons, by God! " Jefferson Dinwoodie muttered as he watched them go. " If you ransacked your many a moon memories, you would discover that Jefferson Dinwoodie didn't ask you to accept his many moons legal services. Damned handsome young couple in many a moon, by God. They must have got off last train to stop here for a day or two. Now, where was I goin'? "

Shifting carefully, Dinwoodie again headed himself in the direction of the three steps that led up to the sheriff's office. He got into motion, not swift motion, but motion of much dignity. He jabbed the needle of memory into his whisky-soaked brain and discovered that he was going to confer with Mr. George Villard—yes, of course, he was going to confer with Mr. Villard. Was he not George Villard's attorney-at-law?

Had he obeyed his small sensible portion of mind, he would have gone up those three steps on hands and knees —but, no sir, he couldn't do that. That would be undignified! He managed to gain the small platform at the head of the steps with but one casualty, though three times he did almost topple over backwards. The single casualty was the ripping of the back seat of his too-tight dingy, black trousers. He managed to get a hold of the jambs of the door, and holding himself used a hand to feel backwards to see whether that rip would cause him to be guilty of indecent exposure.

" No. Got on underclothes," he mumbled. " Don't feel like a long rip. Many a moon! Many a moon! Just bought these pants. Been damned good pants. Goin' to buy a set of new pants."

After resting, perhaps three or four minutes, during which he was watched by a growing, laughing crowd, he got under motion again. He managed to traverse the sheriff's office without mishap. Everywhere there was one chair he saw three and for every table, he saw double. He negotiated the length of the room successfully by dodging the middle table and the middle chair, and gained the entrance of the gloomy jail corridor. Through this doorway he marched grandly, lifting each foot as though it had to clear an obstacle about a foot high.

"Whoopee! Whoopee!" Bill Wallace shouted gleefully, coming out of his grief and frustrated trance. "Here comes your attorney-at-law, George."

"My God, my God," Villard groaned, suddenly enveloped in shame and self-righteousness. "I can't accept the legal advice of a man in that condition. Wallace, the man's drunk!"

"Oh, no, George, he ain't drunk," Wallace corrected and chuckled. "He's only a little tipsy."

"Talk to him, Wallace. Talk to him," Villard ordered. "I can't disgrace myself with trying to converse with a man in his condition. He's drunk."

"Oh, no, George," Wallace vetoed. "I haven't anything to say to him. He's your lawyer. There's the man you want to talk to, Jefferson, right there."

Dinwoodie heard that vaguely because at the moment he was seeing so many barred cells that he had to use the utmost discretion in selecting the one in which his client was imprisoned. All but losing his balance in the effort and retaining it by half falling, half running, he gripped two bars of the cell at the right of the one in which Villard was cooped. He panted for breath, his prominent paunch rubbing against the bars, almost toppling him over backwards, but he clutched the bars as a drowning man would have clutched two straws. He blinked, but when he nodded he bumped his head against a bar and dislodged his hat. It slowly slid off and down his back. He giggled a little because whatever that sliding thing was, it tickled.

"Mishter Wallace," he managed. "Mishter Wallace, come talk to you."

"Yes. I'm Bill Wallace," said the man in the cell. "But I'm not the man you want to talk to, Jeff. He's there to your left. He's George Villard. You know Villainous Villard. He's the man you want to talk to."

"Don't want to talk to Mishter George Villard. Come to talk to you—Bill Wallace. Talked head off to that damned railroad agent, Moreland. He won't listen to reason. Quoted law to him, quoted decisions of subject of demurrage, but the bull-headed son-of-a-bitch won't listen. Mishter Wallace, you got to pay forty dollars a day, many moons, I mean, on those forty empty cattle cars they're holdin' to ship your cattle in—many a moon —forty dollars a day demurrage. Your best way out of this muddle is to pay them thievin' railroad company forty dollars a day demurrage."

"But, damn it, I don't owe any demurrage, Jefferson," Wallace thundered. "I've shipped my cattle. It's Villard there who owes the demurrage. Tell him about it!"

"By drat, he needn't tell me about it. I couldn't understand the drunk man if he did!" Villard snapped. "Demurrage! Demurrage! By the eternal gods, as far as I'm concerned the dratted railroad company can eat its cattle cars, and I'll hold my beef at the home ranch until another railroad company builds a line through here and I can ship on it without bein' imposed upon."

"George, I'm afraid if you do that," Bill Wallace said, "your beef'll get old and tough and stringy. You heard Jefferson's advice, though. You'll have to pay the demurrage."

"Damn drat if I will! I won't pay the railroad company a cent!" Villard thundered. "By the eternal gods, I won't be imposed upon in this matter. Good God, catch the man! Catch the man, he's falling! He's having an apoplectic fit!"

Bill Wallace, actually frightened, tried to hold his breath as the fat and bulky lawyer slowly fell backwards. As Mr. Dinwoodie, now utterly unconscious, reached a horizontal position, his feet shot out from under him and his fat buttocks hit the floor with such a thud that it should have aroused even a drunk man.

"Gosh," Bill Wallace gasped. "I was afraid he'd strike on the back of his head and knock his brains out."

For a few seconds the lawyer's limp and useless legs

waved in the air, then they were outbalanced by his head and his heavy shoulders and he toppled on over, his head making a faint thump as it hit. It also bounced, came to a state of rest.

" But the man's dead! " Villard cried out in fright. " Ain't he dead, Bill? "

" Now, just calm yourself, George, calm yourself," Wallace cried. " He's just drunk."

As an afterthought he added, " He's just good and plenty drunk. He'll be pleadin' your case on demurrage to the railroad company just as soon as he sleeps it off."

George, shivering, pale and frightened, was trying to find suitable words to damn the railroad company and the drunk lawyer when he heard noises in the outer office.

" Is that you, Sheriff Smith? Is that you? " he shouted. " If it is, come on in here and help. Jeff Dinwoodie's dead! He just had an apoplectic stroke! "

" No, he ain't dead, Andy, if that's you," yelled Wallace. " He's just gone out—went out like a candle. Come here and remove his carcass. It's bad enough bein' in jail without havin' to look at him."

It was Andy Smith and he quickly framed himself in the doorway. As Sheriff Smith stared, wondering whether there were any cause for Villard's alarm and fright, he saw that the rectangle of sunlight coming through the barred window centred itself on the fat lawyer's palpitating paunch. A man with such a vibrating belly as that couldn't be dead, not even dying.

Then to the puzzlement of the two prisoners, Sheriff Smith closed and locked the iron door. He next lit a bracket lamp in spite of Villard protesting that it was still daylight.

" Yes, I know that, George," said the sheriff.

Then, to the further puzzlement of the prisoners, the sheriff opened the door of an empty cell, stepped in and came out with the sturdy cot which he had folded together. After he had unfolded it, he pushed it along to a position parallel with the now heavily breathing lawyer.

"But what are you going to do with that, Andy?" Villard panted. "Are you going to use it for a stretcher, and have some other men help you carry him out? I'll help if you'll let me out of here."

"And so will I! So will I!" Wallace declared quickly. "George and me, we can carry him."

Then, after rolling and lighting a cigarette, the sheriff explained that Mr. Jefferson Dinwoodie was not going to be carried out. He was going to be put to bed right here in the jail corridor. Jefferson hadn't done anything to justify his being locked in a cell. He was merely carrying more whisky than he could stand.

"And I'm going to unlock your doors and let you out, friends," the sheriff said confidentially. "You two have got to help me lift Jefferson on to the cot."

"Thank you, thank you, Sheriff," said Villard, when he was out of his cell. "I'll stay out."

"And if that old reprobate stays out, I'll stay out," swore Wallace when he was in the corridor. "He ain't entitled to any more privileges than I am."

"Neither of you are entitled to any privileges," the sheriff told them as his eyes chilled. "You're going to help me lift Jefferson to the cot and then you're goin' back into them cells and stay there. Don't you two forget that you're charged with a felony—that is, if shootin' at each other with a pop gun is a felony. We'll wait till District Judge Green gets here back from Eureka, where he's holdin' fall session, and let him decide that. Come on. Bill, you and me'll get hold of his shoulders and lift and Villard there can handle his feet."

CHAPTER NINETEEN

BIG SAGE was so busy talking about the trouble between Wallace and Villard, serious and humorous, that it paid little attention to the fact that Brazos Cobb and Dobie Dick Donovan were at the Edwards' blacksmith shop. The blacksmith was making for them a running-iron, all of fifteen inches and of three-eighths iron rod, a thing, which when finished, looked like a miniature cane with a curved handle.

"Hey, what are you two doin'?" he demanded in surprise. "Figurin' on oilin' your six-shooters? What are you goin' to do—steal somebody's cattle and then kill the owner if he objects?"

"Yes, that's a possibility, I reckon," replied Brazos, as he swabbed the barrel of his Colt out with a small piece of bandanna. "This here gun of mine, she's gone and got rusted inside her bore."

"Sure, Mr. Edwards, and don't accuse us of such a thing as that," said Dobie Dick. "If you'll keep it a complete secret, we'll tell you why we're 'ilin' and cleanin' these weapons. Do we have your promise?"

Edwards quickly gave his promise.

"You tell him, Brazos," Dobie Dick ordered.

"No, you go ahead and explain to him, Dobie," disagreed Brazos, who did not know what to say.

"Sure, and now here's the way it is, if you keep it a secret, Mr. Edwards," confided Dobie Dick. "We're cleanin' and 'ilin' these pistols to give to Mr. Villard and Mr. Wallace as soon as they're out of jail. It's a duel they're goin' to fight to see which is the better man."

"Donovan, is that the truth?" Edwards demanded suspiciously.

"It's the gospel truth!" Dobie Dick said soberly.

Even as the bewhiskered blacksmith nodded, he was stricken with remorse. He filled his pipe, sat down on the anvil to argue with his conscience. Had he, by this agreement to keep a secret, become an accomplice in a murder—yes, possibly in a double murder, or at least in the death or serious wounding of a rich cattleman? He was immediately so bewildered that he felt as though he wanted to find a priest and confess what he had done, and ask for guidance. He admitted, however, that if one man were to be killed in the coming duel, it would be better suited if George Villard got shot through the heart.

"Damned old hypocrite! He's the hardest man to get money out of all the customers that do business with me on credit. Gettin' a bill out of him is like pullin' a tooth."

Edwards again asked whether they were telling the truth about the proposed duel between the owners of the Circle 22 and the Double W.

"Sure and it's the truth!" said Donovan. "And remember, Mr. Edwards, a secret of it you've got to keep!"

"Damned well he's got to keep it!" Brazos growled. "If he don't I'll drill him!"

"Men, you're foolin', ain't you?" he begged. "You're just talkin' that way to scare me, ain't you?"

They told him emphatically that they were not, and as they told him this, they looked as if nothing would suit them better than to shoot him immediately.

As the blacksmith rehearsed what he'd heard and what he had said, he realised he couldn't so much as tell his wife about it without possibly forfeiting his own life. He'd never been gee-hawed into such a situation as this before. He'd have to be more careful in the future. As he had these thoughts, he remembered that these two men had the reputation of being killers and that they would not shrink from killing him if he broke the promise he had given them.

To make them think he was not distressed, he fished the running-iron out of the slack barrel and let it dry on a gunny sack. As a reminder that he had not yet received the money for the job, he said aloud, but as if to himself:

" It's not a bad job for six bits, includin' the cost of the iron."

" Say, Dobie, who's goin' to pay for this runnin'-iron? " demanded Brazos. " One thing's damned sure—I'm not! "

" And one thing's equally sure—I'm not! " growled Donovan. " By God, it was your scheme, Cobb, and I'm not payin' for your scheme."

They backed away from each other then, two suddenly vicious, deadly men, until they were about fifteen feet apart.

" Now, we'll see who pays for it," Brazos challenged as he slapped his holster.

" And that's fine, Mr. Cobb! " snarled Donovan. " We'll have it this way. The man who dies will pay for the runnin'-iron. Are you agreein' with that, Cobb? "

Before Brazos could reply to that, Edwards told them they could have the job for nothing, provided they would not kill each other in his blacksmith shop.

" All right, all right," Brazos growled. " Maybe it is a better way. We've been cleanin' and oilin' these pistols for Villard and Wallace to kill each other with. Don't you think so, Dobie? "

" No, I don't! " Donovan growled. " Here's the main reason for objectin', Cobb. It's against my principles to accept somethin' for nothin'. How about cuttin' the cards to see who pays for the job? Low card pays. Show us a deck, Edwards."

The blacksmith protested that he did not have a deck of cards short of his house.

" Sure, and how about a dice-box, Blacksmith? " queried Dobie Dick. " Surely in a well-equipped shop like this you've got a dice box."

" Dammit, what do you think I'm runnin'? " Edwards

exploded. "A gamblin' house? Here's what I will do—
I'll go uptown and get a deck of cards for you."

"Oh, no, you won't!" Brazos corrected, making his
small, ugly face deadly.

"And that he will not," agreed Donovan. "He only
wants to take this matter up with the sheriff. Brazos, be
a good boy and take yourself uptown and get us a pack
of cards."

To the surprise of the blacksmith and also Dobie Dick,
Brazos loped away.

Dobie Dick said, as one gentleman confidentially to
another, "Mr. Edwards, if you don't mind tellin' me,
what do you make of that love-makin' business between
Miss Enid Wallace and that Jim Villard. From what has
come to my ears, the majority of their courtin' is done at
your house."

"Well, now, I don't know about it," said Edwards,
much afraid he would say something to offend this gun-
slinger. "Lottie, she's my daughter, she's a close friend
of Miss Enid's, but as for Jim Villard, confidentially,
Dobie, their courtin' around my house is gettin' to be a
damned nuisance."

"Well, now, if you don't mind tellin' me, Mr. Edwards,
do you think their courtin' has reached a point—well,
you know what I mean, have they, so to speak, become
man and wife without the benefit of clergy?"

That puzzled the blacksmith for a few seconds, but
when he got the meaning of it, his bewhiskered face con-
torted with frustrated rage.

"By God, that's what I'm afraid of, Donovan," he
swore, "and if it has come to pass, and there's a scandal
in my house—my wife, she's a good woman, a good,
virtuous, well-meanin' woman—she'll raise hell and put
a chunk under it! Do you think young Villard is capable
of doin' a dirty thing like that—you know what I mean—
takin' advantage of my premises?"

"That young Villard," Dobie Dick said confidentially,
"the young varmint is capable of doin' anything. How

M

about his old man—he'd take somethin' for nothin', wouldn't he?"

"Yes, by George, that's true," Edwards agreed and looked sick. "But here's somethin' I'd like your opinion on, Donovan. Do you think Miss Enid's that kind of a girl?"

"That kind of a girl," Dobie Dick said gravely, "is any kind of a girl, Mr. Edwards, if she is in love with a man like that girl is in love with that scamp, Jim Villard. It's feminine human nature. I'm very much afraid the damage has already been done, Mr. Edwards."

"And so am I," the blacksmith said with a groan.

He forthwith resolved that he'd have to talk with his wife about this, no matter what sort of a storm developed from it. Before he could decide how to open this discussion with his wife, who thought the sun rose and set on Enid Wallace, Brazos arrived with a new pack of cards. He jerked them out of the case, slapped them down on the dirty work bench.

"Shuffle 'em, Dobie! Take out the joker and shuffle 'em."

"Shuffle 'em your damned own self!" snarled Donovan. "Cobb, don't you talk to me thataway. Don't forget I'm a gentleman who is hair-triggered."

"And, by God, so am I!" Brazos snarled, pulling up an end of his mouth. "Donovan, I'm just as hair-triggered as you are and what's more, my gun's been idle for a long time, and when it's idle it itches to go off."

"Let me shuffle 'em for you! Let me shuffle 'em for you!" Edwards panted. "You men act like good friends. I don't want to see trouble between you two."

"Oh, all right," Brazos said, as if he were bitterly disappointed. "That is, if it's all right with Donovan."

"I'll consent to it, but I'd rather not," growled the wagon boss of the Circle 22. "Go ahead and shuffle, Blacksmith, but don't you try a trick."

"Trick? Trick?" Edwards panted. "I don't know how to do a trick with cards."

He shuffled, re-shuffled, shuffled again, possibly shuffled a fourth time, then said, " There you are, men. I assure you I played no trick with those cards."

As Donovan agreed that Brazos cut first, he cut the remaining cards and turned up an ace.

" Ah, I knew I had the luck," chortled Donovan.

" Shut up, you dirty, crowin' bastard! " Brazos Cobb snarled. " If you don't, I'll shoot you."

Then to the surprise, and certainly to the relief, of the blacksmith, Brazos was laughing happily the next moment.

" And I'm a hell of a businessman," he said with self-contempt. " I paid four bits for the cards and bought two drinks uptown, and that cost me two bits, and now I've got to pay six bits for the runnin'-iron. That's a dollar and a half. Dobie, I've got a notion to kill you! "

" Sure, and put your notion off till day after to-morrow," Dobie Dick advised and smiled broadly.

About two minutes later Edwards watched the mis-mated pair head for the main part of town just as friendly as though they were brothers. Forthwith he promised himself that come hell or high water, he was going to tell Sheriff Andy Smith at the first opportunity, and he would make the opportunity. He'd do that if it were the final act of his life. He could do no less and be a good citizen.

In the jail, Villard slewed his cot around in such a position that he could sit down with his back to his fat, heavily breathing lawyer, whose weight threatened to rip the canvas of the rickety cot.

" Ain't a nice thing to look at, is he, George? " Wallace taunted from the adjoining cell. " Sort of makes a finicky man sick, don't he? "

" It's disgusting! " Villard said loudly. " Such a spectacle as he's making now, Bill, is a disgrace on the name of respectable humanity."

" Of which you are the prize example, eh? " laughed

the owner of the Double W. "You sure do love yourself, don't you, George? Say, tell me this, and tell the truth for once in your life. In your own opinion did you ever do a thing that was wrong, or have a thought that was wrong?"

"Yes, I make a mistake occasionally, that is, a mistake in judgment," Villard said with a snort. "But I do believe in respectability, and that thing snoring out there on that cot, sodden drunk, is a blot on all respectability. By drat, I'm going to get out of this jail as quickly as possible. I just won't be humiliated and disgraced by being forced to look at a thing like that."

Wallace reminded him that he was not looking at him. He had his back to the noisily sleeping Jefferson Dinwoodie.

"Drat tarnation, you know what I mean, Wallace!" Villard swore. "I know I ain't lookin' at him, but I can smell him—that's even worse."

"For God's sake, keep still in there, you two fools!" Sheriff Smith yelled from his office. "If you don't, I'll come in there and shoot you both! I've had troublesome prisoners in jail before, many times, but you two skin 'em all! If I hear any more bickerin' and quarrellin' between you two, I'll come in there and tie your tails together and throw you over a clothes-line and let you fight it out. I mean it!"

"I think he means it," Villard whispered reluctantly.

"I know damned well he means it," whispered Wallace. "Me, I'm goin' to stretch out here on this cot and have myself a sleep. Now, don't bother me, Villard, with any more of your fool nonsense!"

At the time Bill Wallace began to snore, which was not more than five minutes after he had stretched out on the hard jail cot, his daughter, sitting on the back steps of the Edwards' home, had her dark head on Jim Villard's shoulder, and he had his left arm about her waist, and Miss Lottie Edwards was watching through the kitchen window.

"Mama, that's the most disgusting thing I ever saw! They're both acting like two love-sick calves."

"Oh, that's all right, Lottie," reassured her mother. "You'll be actin' just like Enid's acting now when the right bull calf comes along."

"I will not! Shame on you, Mama, for making such a comparison as that." But she could not for long keep her eyes from the window. She looked, turned back. "They're kissin' now. That makes it all the more disgusting."

"Yes, disgusting to you now, Lottie," said her mother, who'd learned from experience. "When the right bull calf comes along, you'll be plenty ready to slobber over him."

About three o'clock that afternoon, Blacksmith Edwards, who could not stand worry and anguish any longer, headed for the main part of town, telling himself and not believing it, that he was going up to the Oriental to get a glass of liquor. As the route took him close to the sheriff's office, he looked in, telling himself that he was going to ask Andy Smith to go along with him. He was a little frightened when he saw Smith dozing in his old swivel chair with his boots upon his whittled desk.

Edwards rapped upon the door jamb, and the sheriff awoke with a start, grinned foolishly and said:

"Come on in, Edwards, and we'll chin for a while."

"No, I ain't got the time, Andy," the blacksmith said resolutely. "Come on out. I got somethin' I want to tell you confidential."

"Oh, hell, come on in and tell it to me here! I hear three men snorin' in the jail, which indicates all three are asleep."

"No, come on out. I won't risk it."

Sheriff Smith came out and listened attentively until Edwards had finished telling what he had to say with:

"Andy, you won't let 'em fight that duel, will you?

As sheriff you can't do it, without bein' false to your sworn oath!"

"Then I'll be false to my sworn oath," Andy Smith said savagely. "It'd be the best way for those two fools to settle their trouble. I mean to turn 'em loose day after to-morrow, anyway. Let 'em go to it!"

"But, by God, you wouldn't do that, Andy, would you?" Edwards demanded incredulously.

"Wouldn't I?" said the sheriff with a mirthless chuckle. "You just wait and see, and you look here, Edwards. If you say anything about this, I'll arrest you for bein' an accomplice in this duel fixin' business."

Early the following forenoon, nobody in Big Sage paid any particular attention as Brazos Cobb and Dobie Dick Donovan were seen riding away in the direction of the river ranch of the big Circle 22. Certainly two middle-aged residents of Big Sage, travelling toward each other and meeting in front of the Dodge Brothers' general store, failed to even see those two wagon bosses. One said as they met:

"Jenny, I've got the most scandalous news to tell you, but I've got to tell you in a hurry because I'm on my way in here to get some sugar. I just know that that low-down Jim Villard slept last night at the Edwards' house."

"Oh, that's not news, Hattie," chirruped the other, " I heard that two hours ago. A particular friend of mine —I won't mention names—seen Jim Villard washin' up on the Edwards' back porch a little after daylight this morning. And that awful hypocrite of a Wallace girl, lookin' plenty proud. Did you ever think that low-down Mrs. Edwards would tolerate such goin's on as that— her with a daughter old enough to be married herself? I most certain didn't. I'm goin' to rise up the next time our literary club has its meetin' and make a motion that Edwards woman be dropped as a member. Will you second it?"

"I most certain will! I'll make it if you want me to and you can second it!"

CHAPTER TWENTY

At the river ranch of the Circle 22, Brookins looked with suspicion and no pleasure at scrawny Brazos Cobb. He shot a questioning look at Dobie Dick Donovan. Donovan said that everything was all right. They were after the forty Double W steers.

" He along reppin' for Wallace? "

" Hell, no, he quit Wallace days ago! " Donovan explained. " Him and me have got a little job to do. We want them forty cattle on our own hook. "

The big, hulking straw boss wanted to ask whether they were stealing the cattle, but he lacked the courage, knowing well the deadliness of these two. He did, however, ask whether Wallace were going to ship the forty.

" No, him and Villard are still in jail," said Dobie. " Had a good talk with our boss last night, and we hatched up a plan to hit Wallace below the belt. Got any men to help us cut out them Double W steers, Dave? "

Brookins said he could find several Indians. He did not enthuse about the plan until Dobie Dick and Brazos had explained it fully.

According to their rehearsed lie, they were going to drive the forty steers northward to Flat Mountain and there force them over a tall cliff. It was a cheaper, much more effective way than shooting them. Now Brookins gave his wholehearted approval of the plan, because in his slow-witted mind anything to hurt Bill Wallace was a triumph for the Circle 22. He said that he would have half a dozen riders ready in half an hour.

" While you're gettin' your buckaroos ready, Dave," Donovan said, " I'm goin' to root around and get a sack of grub. Don't mind, do you? "

Brookins certainly did not object to that, as he well knew Donovan's reputation for meanness.

Instead of going to the commissary, Donovan went to an adobe storage shed, where he found a gunny sack. Into this he pushed a large bundle of hogging strings.

Carrying this he entered the bunkhouse, rummaged among his effects. He took a few of his personal belongings, doing this with the belief that he was not coming back.

By three o'clock that afternoon, the nine riders had cut out the steers, and driven them into the sagebrush outside the north line barbed wire fence. Brookins had been warned not to mention the diabolical plan. Consequently he added nothing when Dobie Dick explained to the seven riders that all he and Brazos had wanted was to get Wallace's damned cattle off the Circle 22 river pasture which rightfully belonged to George Villard's cattle.

Donovan ordered the seven riders back to their work. They went without argument.

"And, Dave," said Dobie Dick, as he smiled without any mirth, " if you mention this cattle murderin' business to anybody, I'll come down here and shoot you. Understand what I'm sayin', don't you? "

As soon as the last of the willing helpers were out of sight, Cobb and Donovan began to steer the forty cattle to eastward, keeping just outside the barbed wire fence.

Within half an hour they were thoroughly screened from the headquarters of the Circle 22 and from the spots where any of the Villard men were at work.

They went to work then, not swiftly, but thoroughly, each man on a thoroughly trained horse, and each man well schooled in the handling of his riata. They worked together, not in competition. By the time the sun was sinking below a shoulder of the Two Peaks Range, they had the forty steers thrown and securely hogtied.

"Say, I brought along plenty of hoggin' strings," Dobie Dick chuckled. " Got about thirty left."

Eating some crackers and cheese and canned sardines they had brought from town, they built a small fire of dry willow and sagebrush, and began heating their running-iron.

"There we are, by God," chuckled Brazos about ten o'clock. "He's the last one. Now we'll begin goin' around and turnin' 'em loose. Dobie, you're sure an artist with a runnin'-iron."

"Well, Mr. Cobb, you're not too bad yourself," declared Dobie Dick. "There's a partnership brand—the 4 Diamond. Damned nice brand, ain't it?"

"I never seen a better one, Dobie," Brazos agreed soberly.

As the first flush of day was beginning to shine over the long summit of Flat Mountain, they cut the barbed wire of the Herrit Ranch pastures and drove the cattle through.

Full day had come when they were loosely bunching the forty steers, preparatory to riding into the ranch house to tell Lije Herritt that his beef was ready, when he saw them and rode out.

Lije, as slow-witted as Brookins was, never once thought about where these men had got these cattle. He rode among the steers, nodded as he approved each one. On the Circle 22 stubble and hay, they had put back the weight they had lost.

"Their brands look a little fresh, don't they, boys?" he ventured as he rejoined Dobie and Brazos. "Never saw a brand like that before with four up and down diamonds. Be a hard brand to change, wouldn't it?"

"Now here's how it was, Lije," Dobie Dick Donovan said after he'd put a leg about his saddle-horn. "On his spread, Brazos, he uses two diamonds, and me buyin' in with him, we figured it out we ought to have two more diamonds. Wasn't that what we decided on, Brazos?"

"That's the decision we sure reached, Mr. Donovan," agreed Brazos. "You see my two brands had haired all right and healed over, but when we had to put on two more diamonds to acknowledge that Dobie Dick was my partner, we naturally had to make fresh brands and so everything would look square and upright we draws a runnin'-iron over my old brands. That's why the old brand's so fresh."

To Lije, the brands looked unusual but regular enough. He suggested that as the cattle were safe, they ride in for breakfast.

"Don't care if we do," Brazos agreed, grinning pleasurably. "Dobie and me ain't had nothin' to eat since supper, takin' the whole night to round up these damned steers at Pansy Springs and fetch 'em over here. At Pansy Springs they were scattered out over about four miles."

An hour and a half later they had their stomachs full of good, substantial Herrit food and eleven hundred and fifty dollars of Herrit gold. Brazos asked Lije if he had a small canvas sack for the money.

Fortunately, Lije had one, it being the same one he had carried the gold in from town.

"Now, Lije, if you've got a piece of paper and a pen," said Dobie, "give 'em to me and then you two can go out there and stand in the sunshine and warm up."

He got a sheet of cheap ruled paper and instead of a pen an indelible pencil. The other two went out into the sunshine and stood there talking.

Cobb was called in and asked whether he was ready to sign the memorandum Dobie Dick had written. This memorandum consisted of three words:

"Winner take all."

Under this Dobie Dick Donovan had signed his name with a flourish.

"Want to put your John Hancock down, Brazos?" Dobie Dick asked fraternally.

"Sure, bet your damned life. It'll be hen scratchin', though, but it'll do."

"Sure it'll do, partner," agreed Dobie Dick.

About two hundred yards north of the bridge across the Humboldt there begins a rough S bend in the wagon road. This bend was made necessary by a slough and a short, sharp bend of the river. The road for the entire length of this sharp bend is heavily screened by large, tall, spindly, willows, but at its northerly end and to the right is a hundred yards of open ground between road and river.

"Is this here a good place, Dobie?" Brazos inquired as they stopped their horses. "It suits my fancy all right."

"Just the spot," Dobie Dick said dispassionately. "That is provided you ain't changed your mind, Mr. Cobb, about thinkin' you're a better gun-slinger than I am."

"I ain't changed my mind, Dobie," Brazos said with no show of emotion. "I think I'm the winner and I take all."

"Mr. Cobb, I think you're makin' a mistake."

They rode over the grass, which had been cropped short. They dismounted and dropped their bridle reins. On foot they moved perhaps thirty yards farther. There Brazos placed the canvas sack of money on a dry, flattened gopher mound. Dobie Dick bent, lifted the heavy little sack, placed a sheet of paper under it.

Brazos placed himself just north of the money sack, with his back toward it, and Dobie Dick Donovan backed up a little, looking southward.

"Change your mind, Brazos?"

"Nope! Changed yours?"

"No, Mr. Cobb, here's wishin' you a happy time in hell."

"Don't waste your good wishes, Mr. Donovan," Brazos said with a chuckle. "You're the hombre that's goin' to keep the hell fires goin'. Hope you have a fine journey."

Walking slowly, each took ten steps, stopped. Each, according to their agreement, kept his hand away from his gun.

" And are you ready, Mr. Cobb? " Dobie Dick called over a shoulder.

" Plumb ready! Let her go! "

After the wagon bosses had left, Lije Herritt rode out and took another look at the steers. This time they looked so fine that he decided to ride into Big Sage and tell Brother Ed about them.

Lije Herritt was never a fast or graceful rider, and this time as he thundered into Big Sage, he was riding fast, if ungracefully, and belabouring the flanks of his horse with an ancient quirt.

Stopping his sweating horse at Morton's corner, he shouted, " Say, does anybody know where Andy Smith is? I mean Sheriff Andy Smith? "

Somebody in front of the Oriental Saloon shouted that he'd just seen the sheriff in his office. Lije quirted his horse into a trot, and all but fell as he scrambled from the saddle.

" Be through in just a minute, Lije," the sheriff muttered, and the next moment forgot what he was doing. " My God, Lije, what's wrong now? "

" It ain't much wrong, Andy, it ain't much wrong! " Lije panted. " I just found Brazos Cobb and Dobie Dick Donovan shot to death down there at the other end of the S turn. Must have been they had a duel, because each was shot plumb through the heart. Seems to me each had been shot two times. I examined their guns, Andy, two empty shells in each gun."

" I see," said the sheriff, suppressing his amazement. " What's that you've got in your hand, Lije? "

" Oh, that, that," Lije said. " It was on an old gopher mound right between 'em."

He trotted forward and laid the money sack and the sheet of crumpled paper on the sheriff's desk. The sheriff smoothed out the paper, read it and raised his eyes.

" What's the meanin' of this, Lije? "

"Meanin' of that? I didn't read it," Lije shouted. "This here money bag, it contains eleven hundred and fifty dollars I paid for them forty head of cattle. Bought 'em from Brazos Cobb and Dobie Dick Donovan. Was ridin' in to tell Ed about what a good deal I made when I run across them dead men. When they left my ranch they was fine friends—laughin' and jokin' and talkin' with one another."

"Yeah, fine friends. They hated each other. Lije, do you know what's written on this paper?"

"No, I don't, read it, Andy."

"It says," growled the sheriff, "'Winner take all,' and under 'Winner take all' are the signed names of Brazos Cobb and Dobie Dick Donovan. You see, it was a gamblin' game, each man stakin' his life, and they both lost. It ain't a big loss for this part of Nevada."

"It was a gamblin' game?" cried Lije so loud that he shook Bill Wallace and George Villard out of their brooding and vengeful reverie. They shouted, demanding to be told what was wrong—in particular, demanding to be told whether at last they were going to be released, so they could get real guns and shoot it out.

Lije Herritt, motivated by fright and horror to super speed, left at a lope to tell brother Ed and the town about the double tragedy. Sheriff Andy Smith slowly dragged open the iron door and slowly went into the jail corridor, where his two prisoners were still clammering for an explanation.

"For God's sake, keep still, you two!" the sheriff snapped. "This don't concern you at all. Dobie Dick and Brazos Cobb just a little while ago killed each other just beyond the double turn, the other side of the bridge. Lije Herritt, he fetches in the news."

"My God, my God," Villard groaned, as he realised what the sheriff had said. "I've lost the best wagon boss in Nevada."

"No, you ain't," Bill Wallace corrected. "I'm the

one who should weep. Brazos Cobb was the best damned wagon boss as ever forked a saddle."

They were starting to make this a real squabble when the sheriff stopped them with an oath, telling them that if they didn't quit acting like fools, he'd keep them in jail for ten years. They dropped weakly back to their cots.

" And unless my hunch is dead wrong, Bill," the sheriff went on, " I think I've got a bag of money in there that belongs to you. Accordin' to Lije, he bought forty steer from Cobb and Donovan branded four Diamonds. I don't know of any such brand. It could have been worked out of the Double W all right."

" Why, the damned cattle thieves! " Wallace swore as he stiffened.

Villard started to laugh, changed his mind, because with the loss of the forty Double W steers he had no chance to collect for pasturage. He demanded details, but before the sheriff could begin to tell everything he knew and thought, in rushed about forty people, an excited congregation led by Jim Villard and Enid Wallace. They were breathing hard, wearing the same good clothes they had worn the day before.

" Drat it, Jim, drat it! " Villard swore as he scrambled to his feet. " Quit associatin' with that girl."

" And Enid," Wallace ordered as he got to his feet, " keep away from that young feller! He ain't no good. It's the last time I'm goin' to tell you! Keep away from him, or he'll get you into trouble! "

Though men, and a few women, were demanding to be told whether there were any truth in the report that Dobie Dick Donovan and Brazos Cobb had killed each other, the sheriff, by waving his arms and yelling, managed to make himself heard.

" Now, you two old fools, keep your shirts on and be quiet! " he ordered. " As for Jim and Enid, there ain't two finer young people in the sagebrush country, and besides, if your fine morals are all shaken up, they've been married for two days. Ain't a man got a right to bring his wife into my jail to call on his father and her father?"

"They're married!" croaked George Villard as he stared blankly. "Why, this can't be true."

"Them two are married, and been married for two days?" muttered Bill Wallace as he stared at his almost tearful daughter and the grim faced young man at her side. "Villard, you ornery old reprobate, do you know what we should do?"

"Yes, yes, what should we do, Bill?" Villard whispered shakily. "I ain't quite myself right now. What do you advise we do?"

As though they spoke quietly, they moved to the line of bars that separated their cells. There they stopped, stiffened, Villard the stiffer. He tried to smile and had a suspicion of success at it.

Bill Wallace was now grinning sheepishly, though he wanted to swear loud enough to be heard all the way to the shipping pens.

"Well, what about it, George?" he demanded, unwilling to make the next move. "If they're really married, there ain't much we can do about it, is there?"

"No, there ain't, Bill," George Villard confessed and actually chuckled. "You'll oblige me if you'll let me shake your hand.

"Huh!" Wallace snorted. "We're actin' like a pair of blamed old fools without half an ounce of brains in both our heads. Here, shake!"

They shook and shook hard, but the next moment wildly gestured while they told the sheriff they should rightfully be liberated.

"Sure, I'm goin' to let you old fools out," the sheriff agreed, as he fumbled for his keys. "But, George, I'm goin' to let you out on one condition. That is, you'll kiss the bride like you meant it. I've known for two days these two were married—you two and your fine morals! Seems to me if you two do what you ought to do, you'd go down yonder beyond the bridge and finish your fightin' like Dobie Dick Donovan and Brazos Cobb did."

"No, no, Smith, no, no!" Villard said loudly and tearfully. "Open our cell doors, Andy, and I'll take this sweet girl to my breast as if she were my real daughter."

"You damned well better!" Bill Wallace growled under his breath, as he waited trembling and eager to be liberated.

THE END